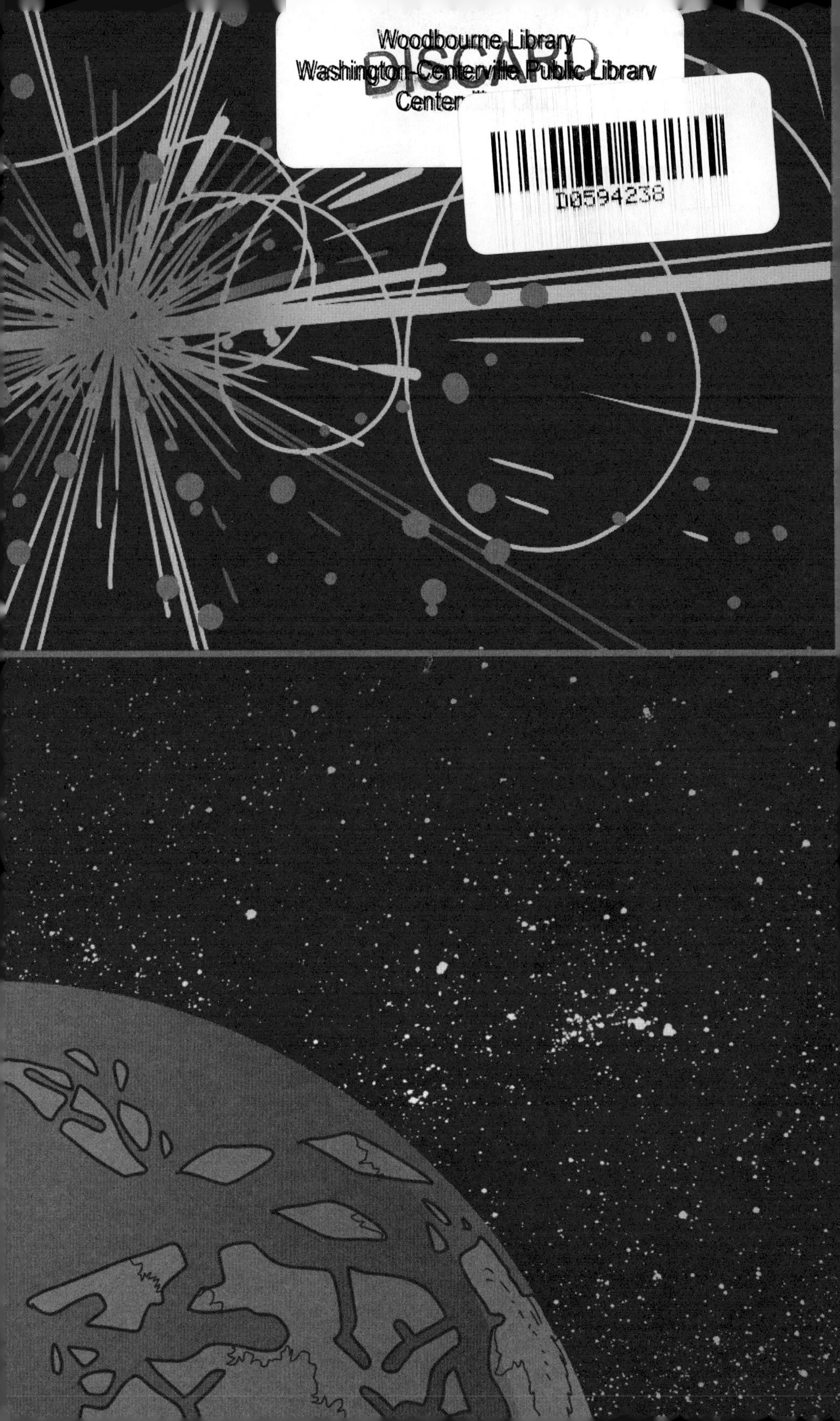

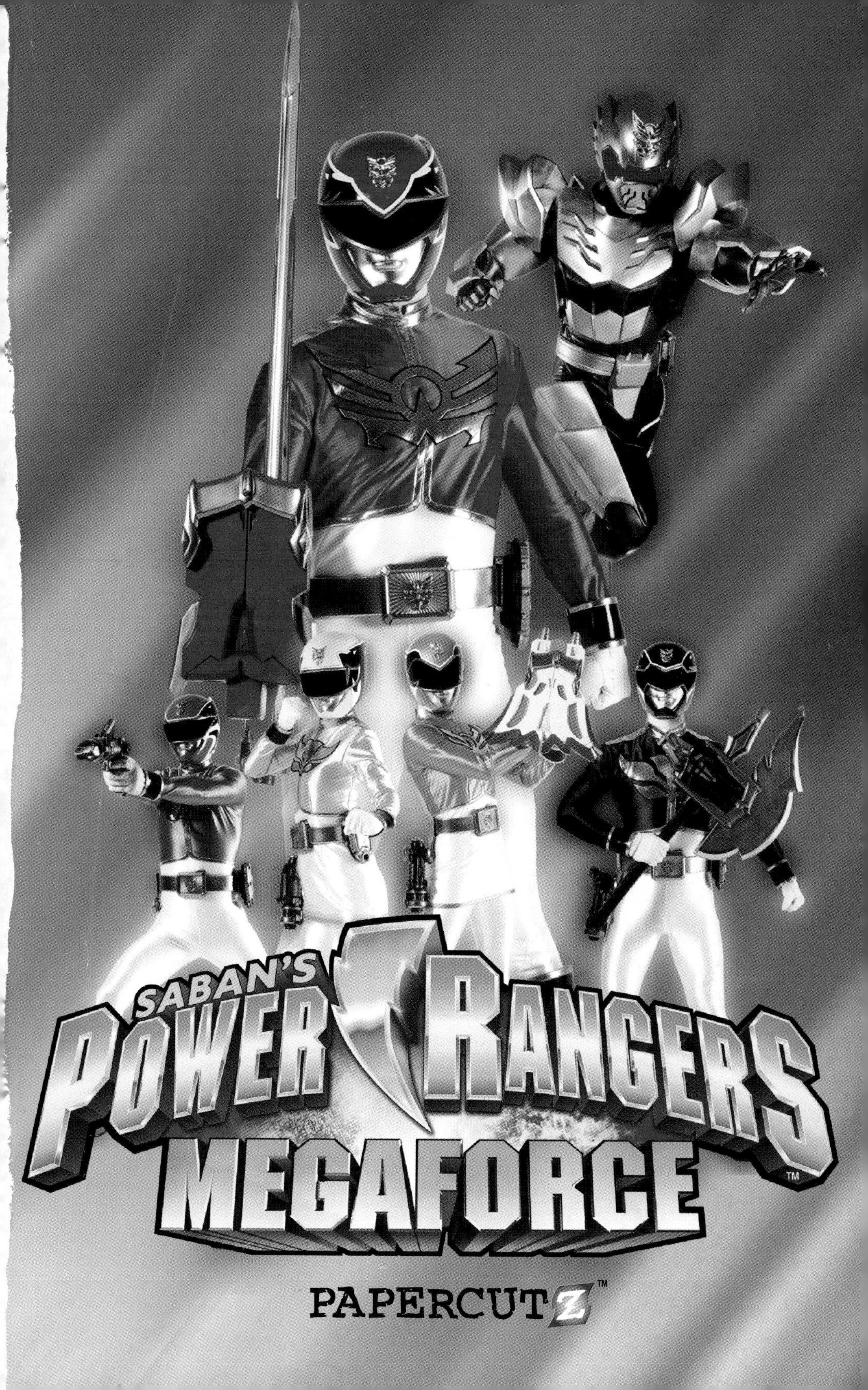

SABAN'S POWER RANGERS MEGAFORCE™

PAPERCUTZ™

SABAN'S POWER RANGERS

Graphic Novels Available From PAPERCUTZ

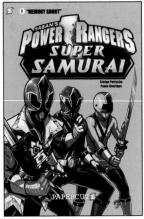

1 "MEMORY SHORT"
SABAN'S POWER RANGERS SUPER SAMURAI
Stefan Petrucha
Paulo Henrique
PAPERCUTZ

Graphic Novel #1

2 "TERRIBLE TOYS"
Stefan Petrucha • Paulo Henrique
SABAN'S POWER RANGERS SUPER SAMURAI
PAPERCUTZ

Graphic Novel #2

3 "PANIC IN THE PARADE"
SABAN'S POWER RANGERS MEGAFORCE
"GAME ON!"
PAPERCUTZ

Graphic Novel #3

4 "BROKEN WORLD"
Stefan Petrucha • PH Marcondes
SABAN'S POWER RANGERS MEGAFORCE
PAPERCUTZ

Graphic Novel #4

Coming Soon

RITA REPULSA'S ATTITUDE ADJUSTMENT
Stefan Petrucha
PH Marcondes
SABAN'S MIGHTY MORPHIN POWER RANGERS
THEY'RE BACK!
PAPERCUTZ

Mighty Morphin Power Rangers
Graphic Novel #1

POWER RANGERS graphic novels are available for $6.99 each in paperback, and $10.99 in hardcover except volume 4 and MIGHTY MORPHIN POWER RANGERS #1, $7.99pb/$11.99hc. Available at booksellers everywhere. You can also order online from www.papercutz.com. Or call 1-800-886-1223, Monday through Friday, 9 – 5 EST. MC, Visa, and AmEx accepted. To order by mail, please add $4.00 for postage and handling for first book ordered, $1.00 for each additional book and make check payable to NBM Publishing. Send to: Papercutz, 160 Broadway, Suite 700, East Wing, New York, NY 10038.

SABAN'S POWER RANGERS MEGAFORCE ™

❹ "BROKEN WORLD"

Stefan Petrucha – Writer

PH Marcondes – Artist

Laurie E. Smith– Colorist

PAPERCUTZ ™
New York

SABAN'S POWER RANGERS MEGAFORCE
#4 "BROKEN WORLD"

STEFAN PETRUCHA -- Writer
PH MARCONDES -- Artist
LAURIE E. SMITH -- Colorist
BRYAN SENKA -- Letterer

UMESH PATEL (RANGER CREW) -- Special Thanks
KAY OLIVER & MARY RAFFERTY -- Extra Special Thanks
DAWN K. GUZZO -- Production
BETH SCORZATO -- Production Coordinator
MICHAEL PETRANEK -- Editor
JIM SALICRUP
Editor-in-Chief

ISBN: 978-1-59707-392-9 paperback edition
ISBN: 978-1-59707-393-6 hardcover edition

Printed in China
December 2013 by New Era Printing LTD.
Unit C. 8/F Worldwide Centre
123 Chung Tau, Kowloon
Hong Kong

Papercutz books may be purchased for business or promotional use. For information on bulk purchases please contact
Macmillan Corporate and Premium Sales Department at (800) 221-7945 x5442.

Distributed by Macmillan

First Printing

MEET SABAN'S POWER RANGERS MEGAFORCE™

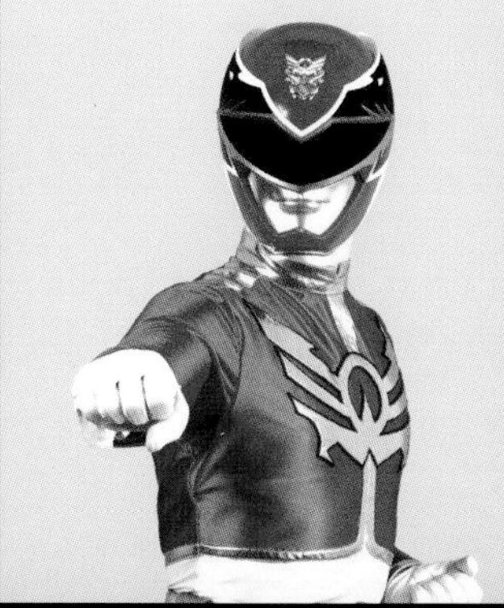

For centuries, the Earth has been protected by a supernatural guardian being named Gosei and his robotic aide, Tensou. When the evil Warstar aliens begin their massive invasion, Gosei calls upon five teenagers to form the ultimate team...
the Power Rangers Megaforce!

Using their newfound abilities, mega-weapons, tech Zords and Megazords, the fate of the world rests in the hands of the Power Rangers Megaforce.

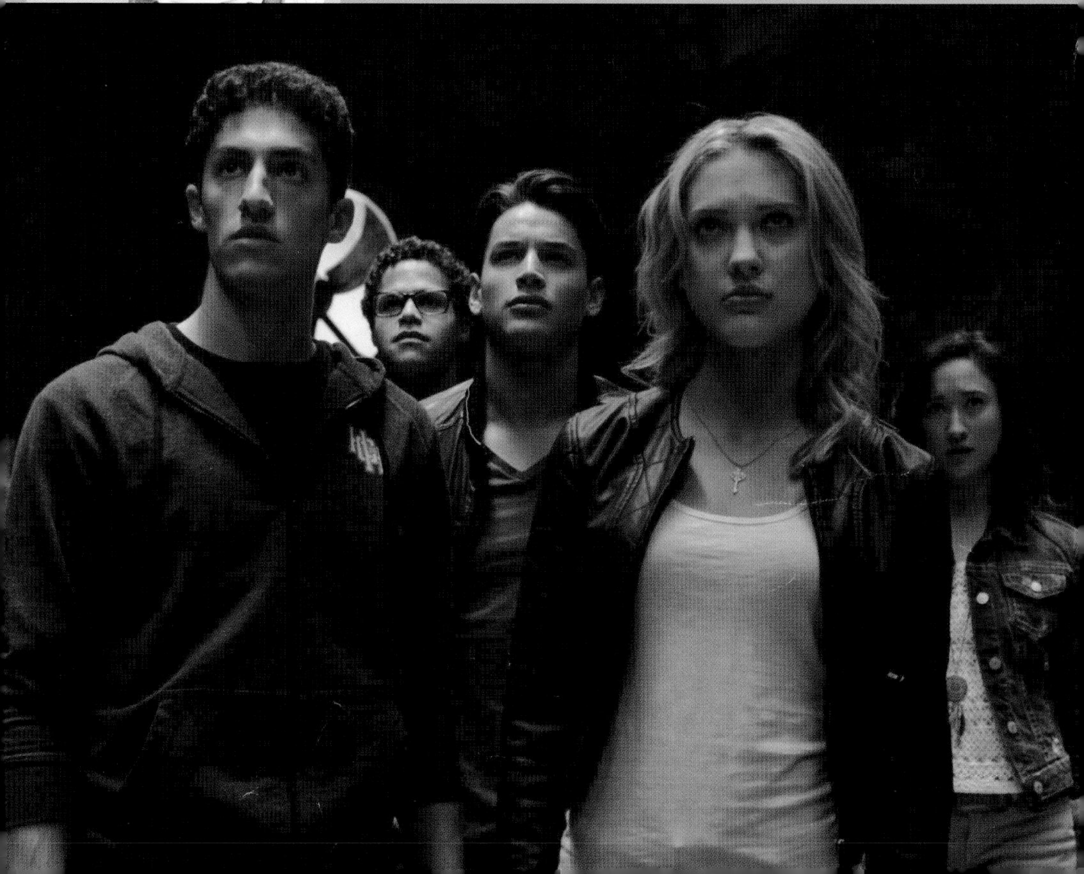

THE RED RANGER (TROY BURROWS)

Troy finds himself as the new kid in town... again. Moving often has made Troy grow up fast, as he had to quickly learn how to take care of himself. Troy is a bit of a loner, but he's eager to make friends in his new hometown. His life, however, is about to take an unexpected turn.

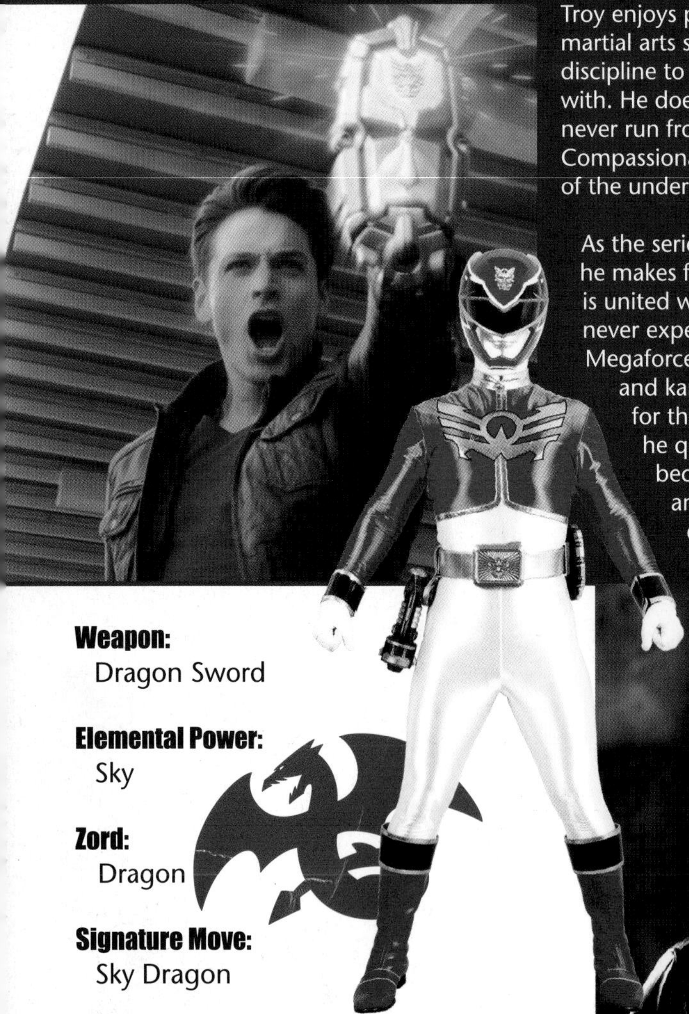

Troy enjoys practicing and perfecting his martial arts skills. He's got the focus and discipline to make him a force to be reckoned with. He doesn't look for trouble but he'll never run from it when someone is in need. Compassionate and loyal, Troy is a champion of the underdog be they human or alien.

As the series begins, Troy is grateful when he makes friends with the other teens and is united with them as the Megaforce. Troy never expected to be the leader of the Megaforce, but with his manner, discipline, and karate skills, it's as if he were training for the job all his life. A natural leader, he quickly rises to the challenge of becoming the newest Red Ranger and leading his comrades into every skirmish with courage and determination.

Weapon:
Dragon Sword

Elemental Power:
Sky

Zord:
Dragon

Signature Move:
Sky Dragon

Notes:
It's his destiny to lead the Megaforce.

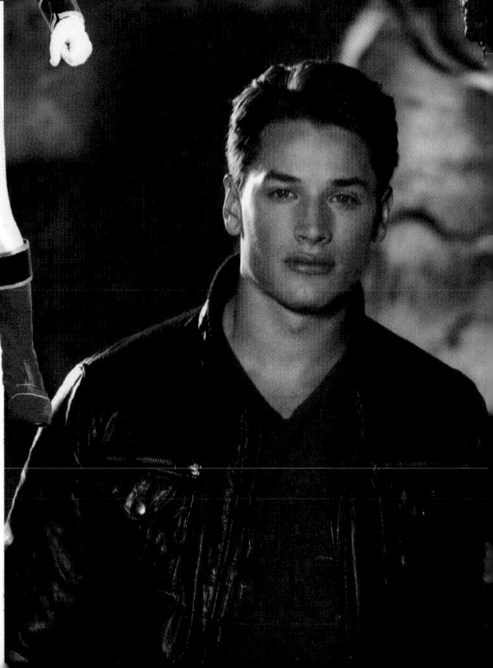

SABAN'S POWER RANGERS MEGAFORCE

THE PINK RANGER (EMMA GOODALL)

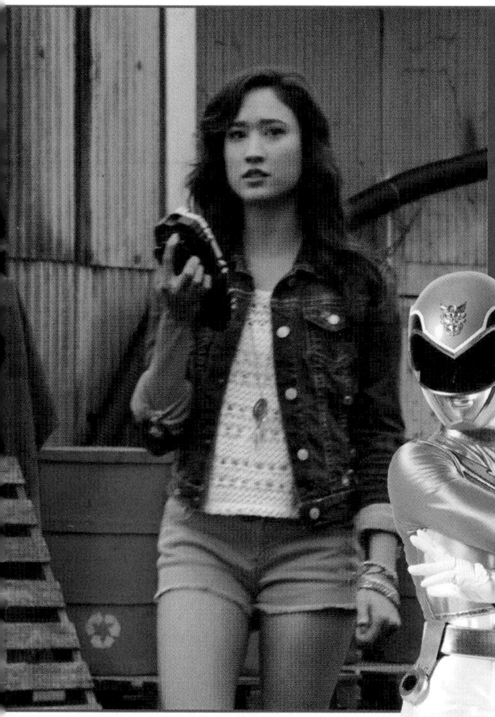

Emma is a compassionate and charitable teen who will do what it takes to protect the environment. While photography is a great way for Emma to express her love of nature, her more wild side has a desire to be a BMX biker.

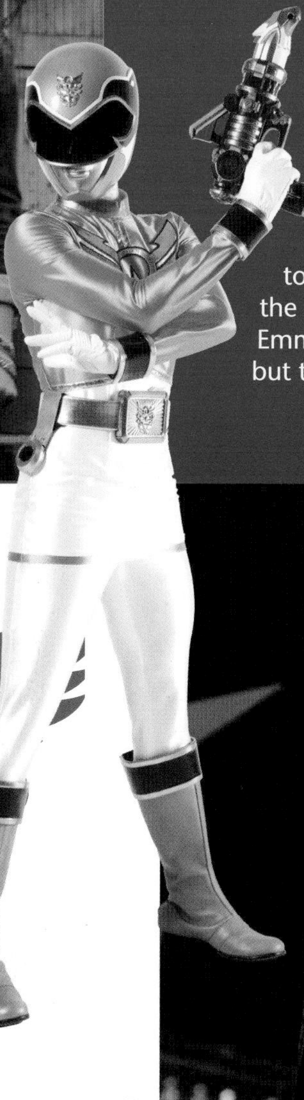

Surprised like the rest of the Ranger team when called upon to be part of the Megaforce, Emma takes the alien attacks on the environment personally and is anxious to protect the world. As the Pink Ranger, not only is it Emma's goal to save the world, but to make it a better place.

Weapon:
Phoenix Flare

Elemental Power:
Sky

Zord:
Phoenix

Signature Move:
Air Phoenix

Notes:
Emma is a skilled BMX cyclist.

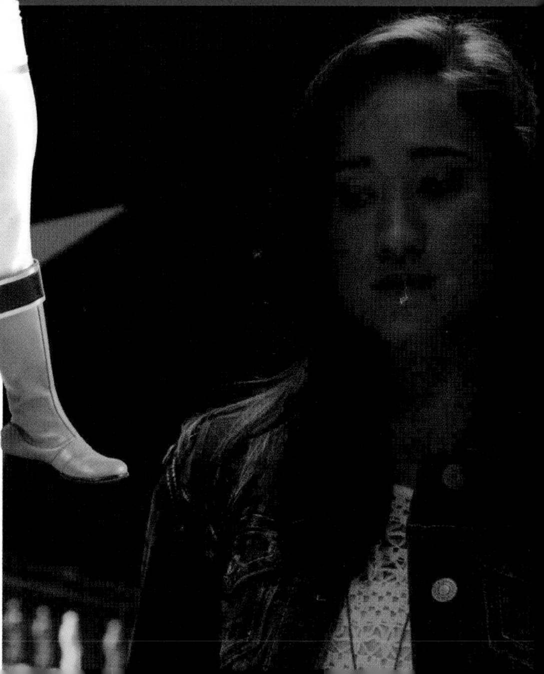

THE BLUE RANGER (NOAH CARVER)

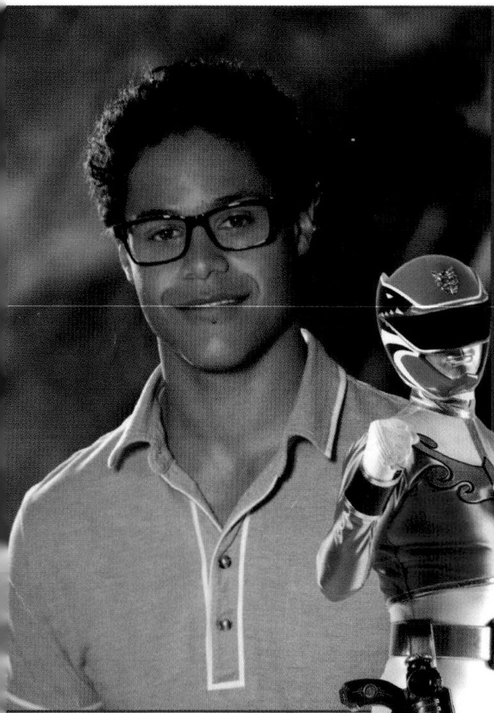

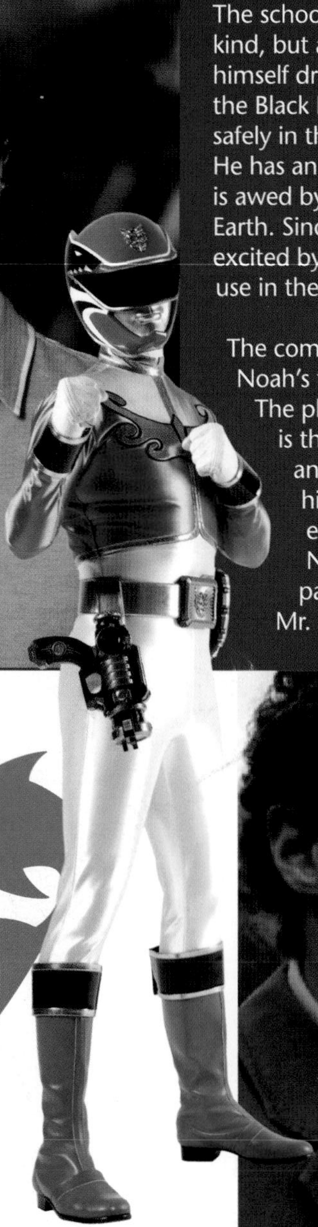

The school's geek, Noah is incredibly clever and kind, but a bit socially akward. He often finds himself dragged into social adventures by Jake, the Black Ranger, when he would rather remain safely in the warm glow of a computer monitor. He has an insatiable thirst for knowledge and is awed by the fact that aliens are attacking the Earth. Since becoming a Ranger, he is even more excited by the technology that the team gets to use in their battles.

The combination of Jake's social savvy and Noah's tech skills make them a great team. The physical part of being a Power Ranger is the hardest part for Noah but with Troy and Jake being at his side, they encourage him to try. In the end, Noah succeeds by employing his true strength-- brainpower. Noah shares his love of science and the paranormal with his goofy science teacher, Mr. Burley.

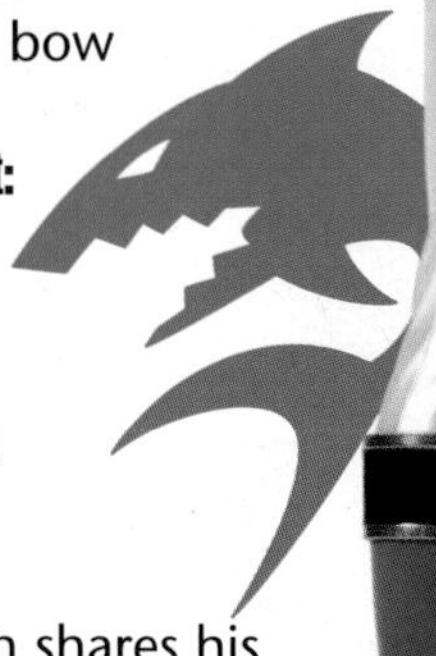

Weapon:
Shark bow

Element:
Sea

Zord:
Shark

Notes:
Noah shares his love of the paranormal with his science teacher, Mr. Burley.

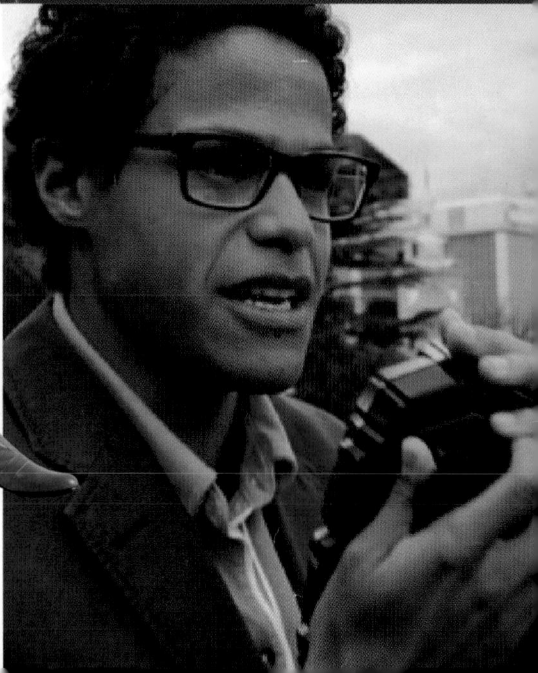

THE YELLOW RANGER (GIA MORAN)

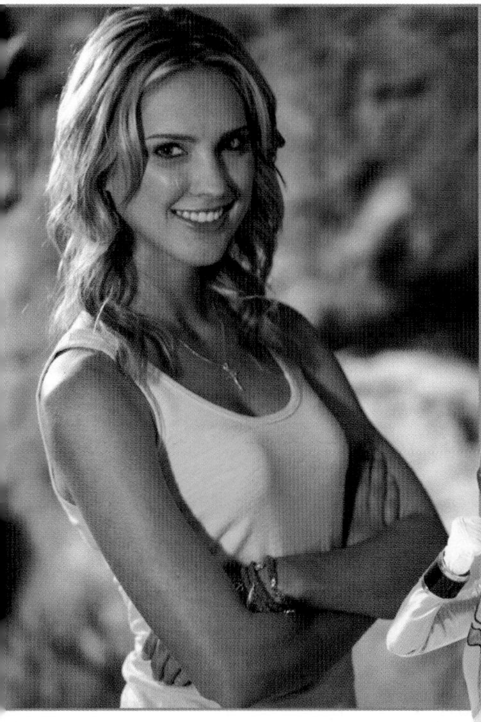

Gia is beautiful, smart and a formidable martial artist with a generally unflappable demeanor. Not only is she the prettiest and most intelligent girl at school, she is also the toughest. While her personable manner tempts many boys, her martial art skills keep them at bay. Gia carries herself with a sense of confidence that comes from success.

She is loyal to her friends and is best friends with Emma, the Pink Ranger. They have known each other since they were little girls and have remained friends even though they are now very different.

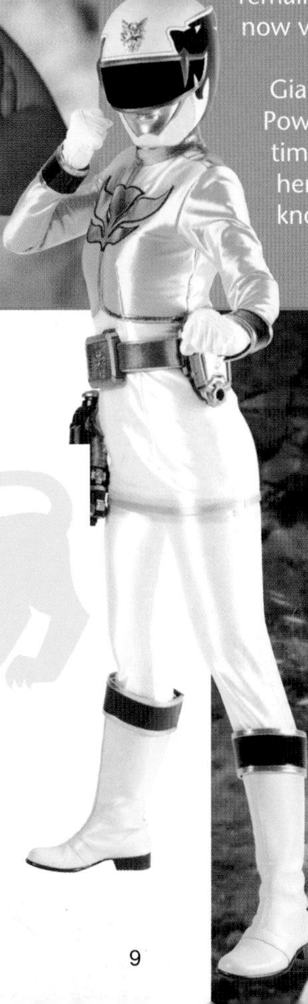

Gia is the perfect addition to the Power Rangers team even though at times her effortless success furstrates her new teammates, but everyone knows they can count on her.

Weapon:
Tiger Claw

Element:
Earth

Zord:
Tiger

Notes:
Jake (the Black Ranger) has a crush on her.

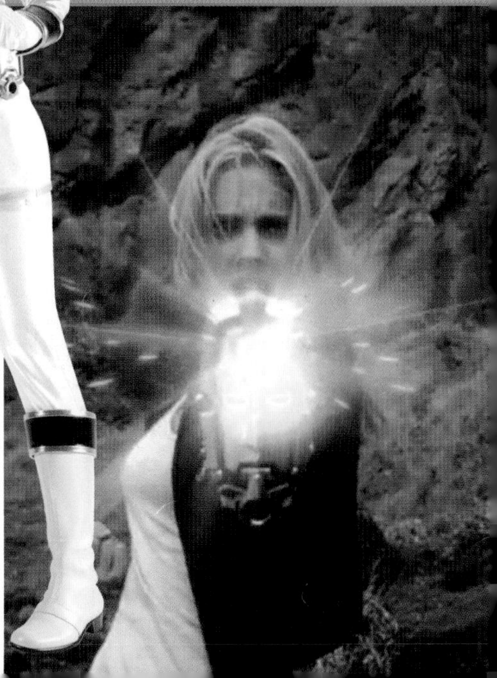

SABAN'S POWER RANGERS MEGAFORCE

THE BLACK RANGER (JAKE HOLLING)

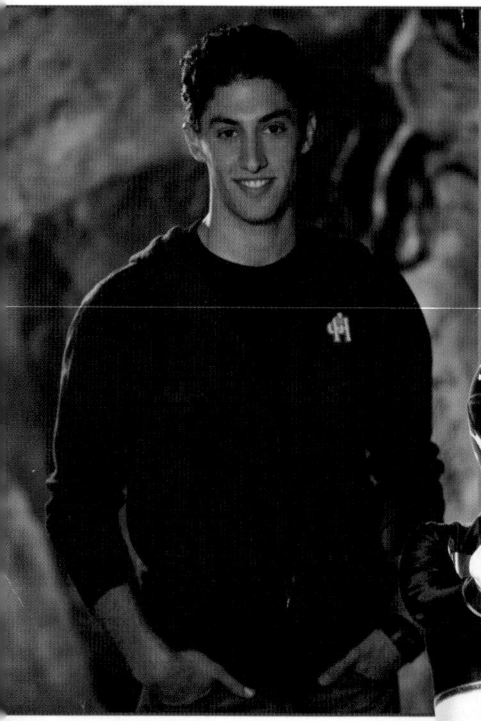

Jake is a fearless, fun-loving teen with a never-ending well of optimism. His athletic abilities are good enough to make the team, but not be the star player. His main passion in life is soccer and it's rare to find him without a soccer ball nearby. Jake's fearlessness also applies to his social life. His determination will not allow something like the lack of an invitation to stop him from going to a party or getting out on the dance floor.

He is best friends with Noah, the Blue Ranger, whom he never stops trying to get to loosen up and have some fun. Jake sees his new super-hero role as an opportunity to do great things even if he occasionally wishes he could let the world know that he's the one saving it. Jake does have one major weak spot and that's his crush on Gia, the Yellow Ranger. He tries to play things cool but he wears his heart on his sleeve and he's certain that one day he'll win her over.

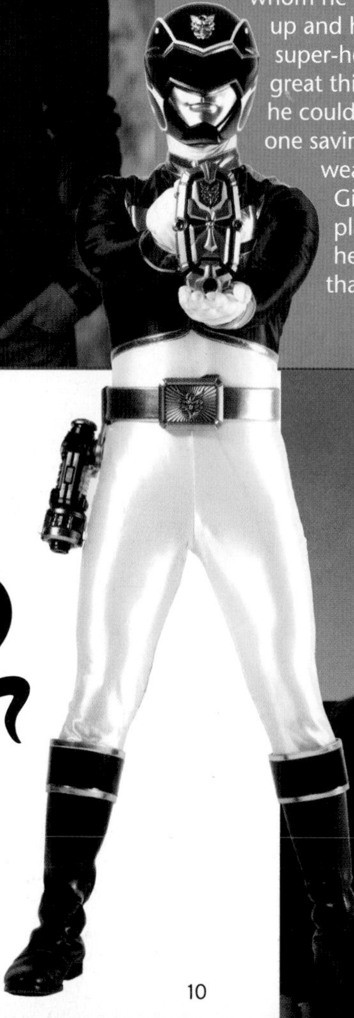

Weapon:
Snake Axe

Elemental Power:
Earth

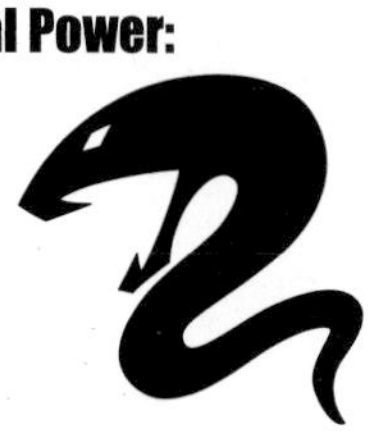

Zord:
Snake

Notes:
Jake is an excellent soccer player, and often has a ball with him.

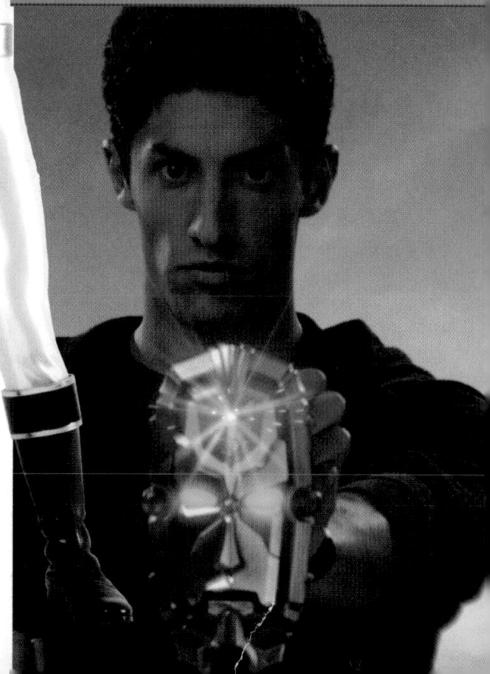

SABAN'S POWER RANGERS MEGAFORCE

ROBO KNIGHT

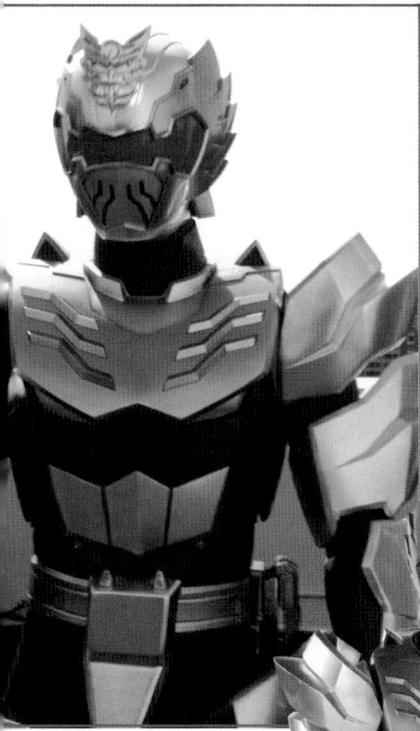

When the Rangers are in the battle for their lives, suddenly there appears an unknown Ranger wearing the same Gosei symbol. The Rangers instantly know he is a part of the Power Rangers. Robo Knight was created by Gosei centuries ago to protect the Earth at all costs. He is powered by the Earth's own elements and he can call on those same elements to use as his powers.

Robo Knight, however, had been buried for centuries and only recently awakened when the Earth sensed danger. The long sleep affected many portions of his memory and now there are times he sees humans as the greatest threat to the Earth. The Power Rangers slowly remind him that there are great attributes to be human and that the Power Rangers see Robo Knight as a good friend-- something he had long forgotten. Unlike the Rangers who have to call their Zords, Robo Knight has the unique ability to morph into his Lion Zord and back again to a robot. A power the Rangers witness firsthand.

Robo Knight learns that humanity's fate is intertwined with Earth's and both are worth saving.

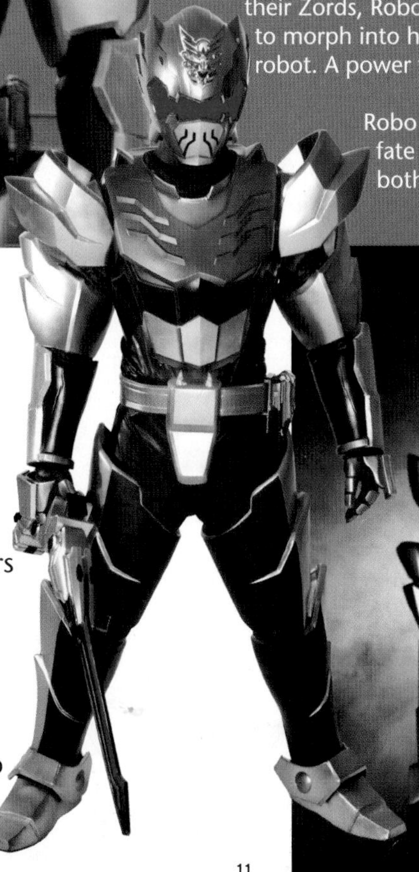

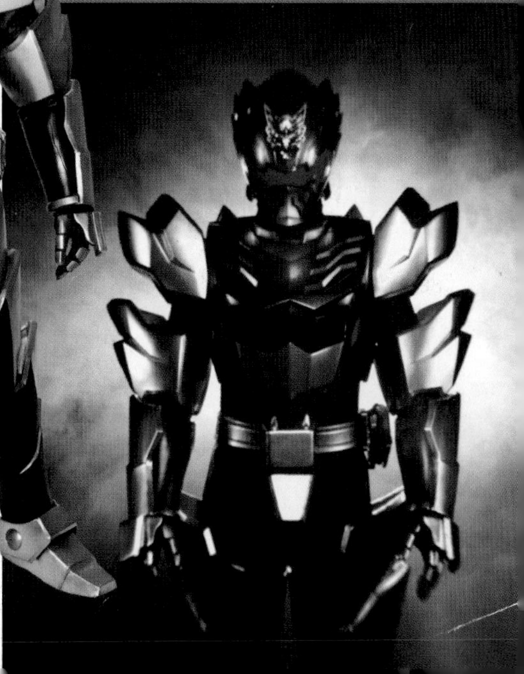

Weapon:
Robo Blaster and Robo Blade

Element:
Access to all Elemental Powers

Zord:
Lion

Notes:
He is the de facto sixth ranger.

SABAN'S POWER RANGERS MEGAFORCE

ADMIRAL MALKOR

Admiral Malkor is the moth-like commander of the Warstar ship, and the leader of the alien attack force. His goal is to make the Insectoids rule the Earth, and for humans to be nothing but a distant memory. He does not tolerate failure.

VRAK

Vrak is not an Insectoid-- he is a member of the alien royal family, and brother to the prince who commands the imminent invasion. He is unique with special powers not possessed by the Insectoids, and seeks to one day use his intelligence to rule over the other aliens, and become emperor.

CREEPOX

The hulking Insectoid lieutenant that serves at Malkor's side, Creepox, believes firmly in insect superiority. He would like nothing more than to unleash a full-scale attack on planet Earth, and is obsessed with defeating the Red Ranger in one-on-one combat.

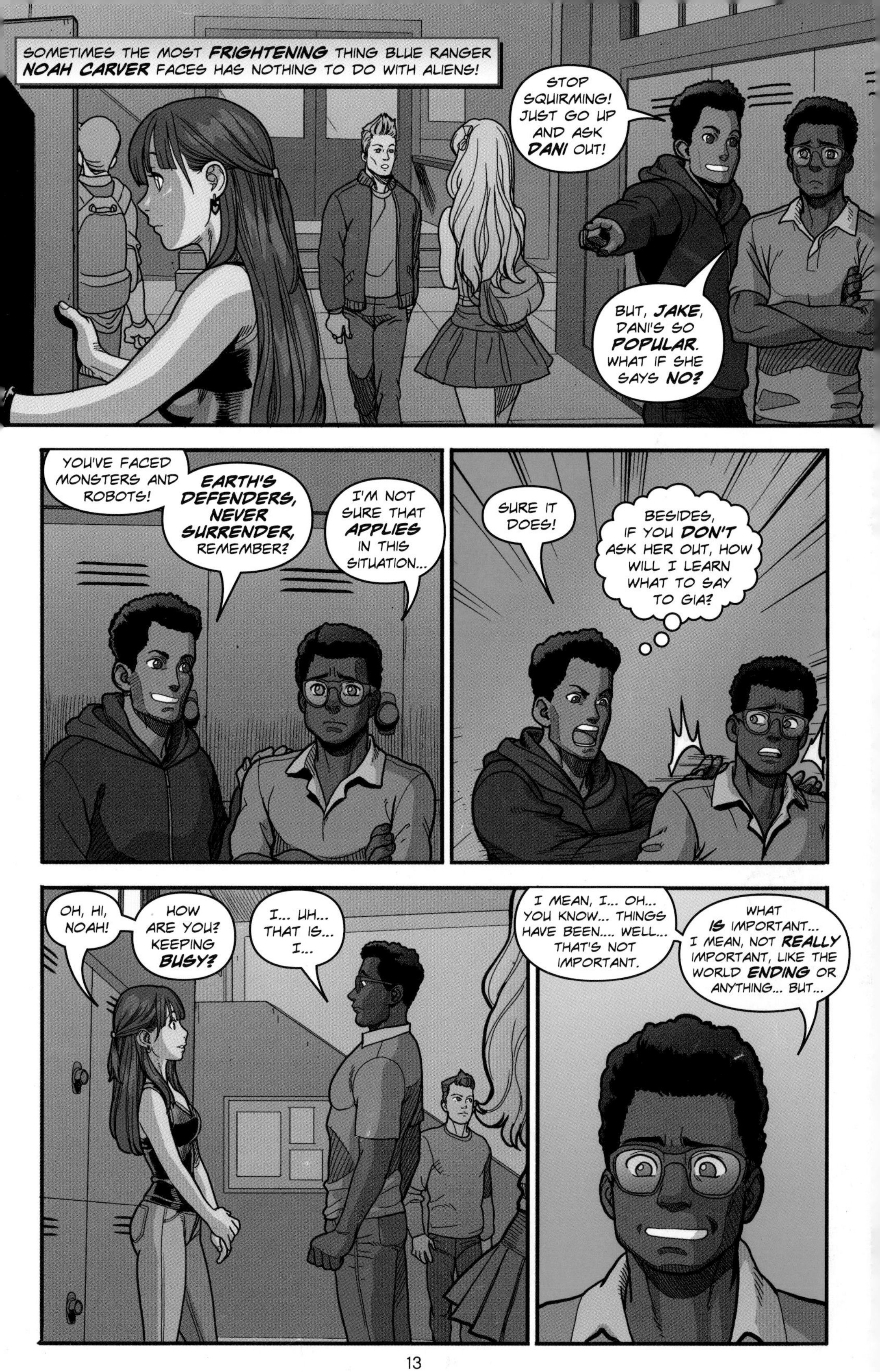
SOMETIMES THE MOST FRIGHTENING THING BLUE RANGER NOAH CARVER FACES HAS NOTHING TO DO WITH ALIENS!
STOP SQUIRMING! JUST GO UP AND ASK DANI OUT!
BUT, JAKE, DANI'S SO POPULAR. WHAT IF SHE SAYS NO?
YOU'VE FACED MONSTERS AND ROBOTS!
EARTH'S DEFENDERS, NEVER SURRENDER, REMEMBER?
I'M NOT SURE THAT APPLIES IN THIS SITUATION...
SURE IT DOES!
BESIDES, IF YOU DON'T ASK HER OUT, HOW WILL I LEARN WHAT TO SAY TO GIA?
OH, HI, NOAH!
HOW ARE YOU? KEEPING BUSY?
I... UH... THAT IS... I...
I MEAN, I... OH... YOU KNOW... THINGS HAVE BEEN.... WELL... THAT'S NOT IMPORTANT.
WHAT IS IMPORTANT... I MEAN, NOT REALLY IMPORTANT, LIKE THE WORLD ENDING OR ANYTHING... BUT...

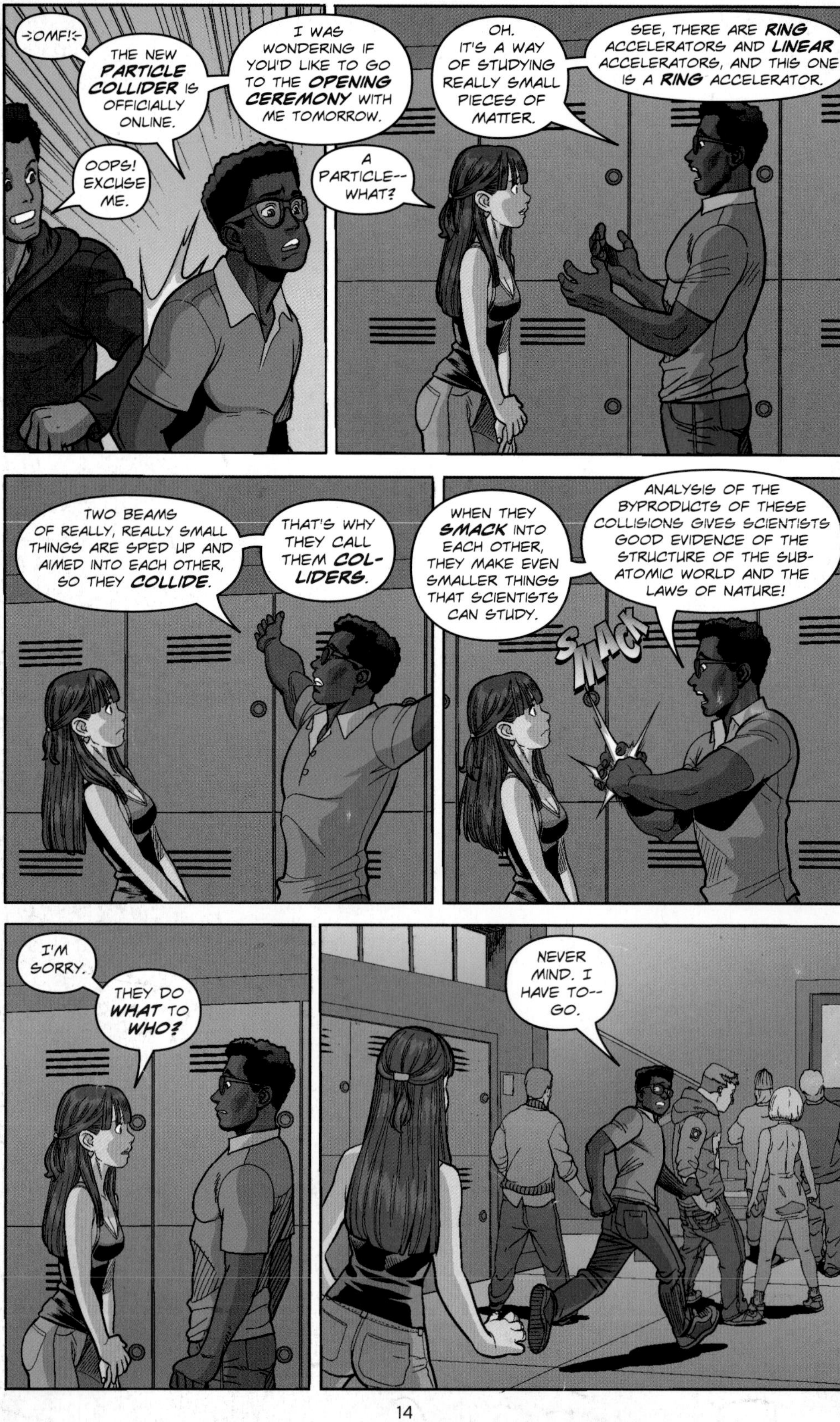

OMF!
THE NEW PARTICLE COLLIDER IS OFFICIALLY ONLINE.
OOPS! EXCUSE ME.
I WAS WONDERING IF YOU'D LIKE TO GO TO THE OPENING CEREMONY WITH ME TOMORROW.
A PARTICLE--WHAT?
OH. IT'S A WAY OF STUDYING REALLY SMALL PIECES OF MATTER.
SEE, THERE ARE RING ACCELERATORS AND LINEAR ACCELERATORS, AND THIS ONE IS A RING ACCELERATOR.
TWO BEAMS OF REALLY, REALLY SMALL THINGS ARE SPED UP AND AIMED INTO EACH OTHER, SO THEY COLLIDE.
THAT'S WHY THEY CALL THEM COL-LIDERS.
WHEN THEY SMACK INTO EACH OTHER, THEY MAKE EVEN SMALLER THINGS THAT SCIENTISTS CAN STUDY.
ANALYSIS OF THE BYPRODUCTS OF THESE COLLISIONS GIVES SCIENTISTS GOOD EVIDENCE OF THE STRUCTURE OF THE SUB-ATOMIC WORLD AND THE LAWS OF NATURE!
SMACK
I'M SORRY.
THEY DO WHAT TO WHO?
NEVER MIND. I HAVE TO--GO.

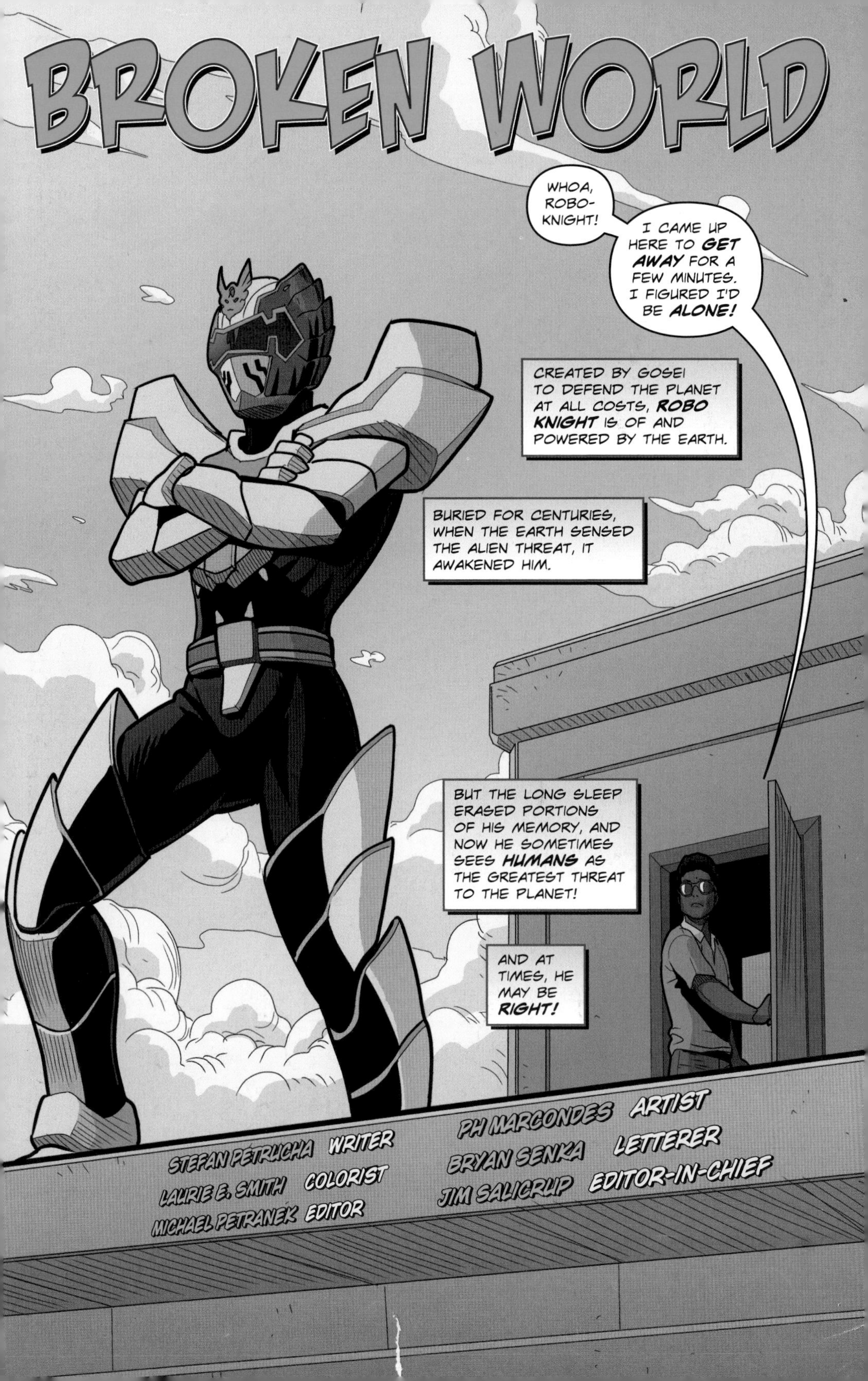
BROKEN WORLD
WHOA, ROBO-KNIGHT!
I CAME UP HERE TO GET AWAY FOR A FEW MINUTES. I FIGURED I'D BE ALONE!
CREATED BY GOSEI TO DEFEND THE PLANET AT ALL COSTS, ROBO KNIGHT IS OF AND POWERED BY THE EARTH.
BURIED FOR CENTURIES, WHEN THE EARTH SENSED THE ALIEN THREAT, IT AWAKENED HIM.
BUT THE LONG SLEEP ERASED PORTIONS OF HIS MEMORY, AND NOW HE SOMETIMES SEES HUMANS AS THE GREATEST THREAT TO THE PLANET!
AND AT TIMES, HE MAY BE RIGHT!
STEFAN PETRUCHA WRITER
LAURIE E. SMITH COLORIST
MICHAEL PETRANEK EDITOR
PH MARCONDES ARTIST
BRYAN SENKA LETTERER
JIM SALICRUP EDITOR-IN-CHIEF

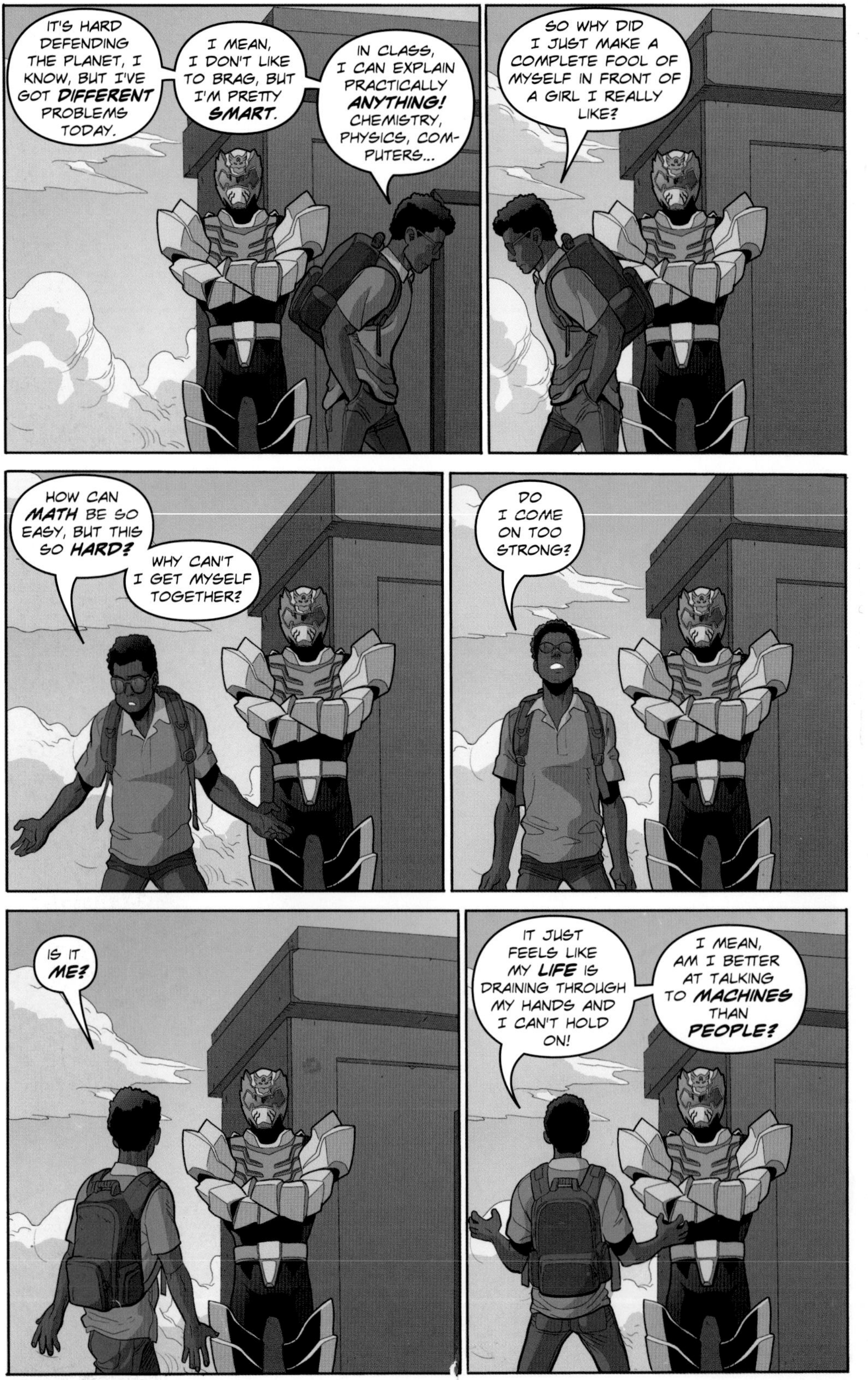
IT'S HARD DEFENDING THE PLANET, I KNOW, BUT I'VE GOT DIFFERENT PROBLEMS TODAY.
I MEAN, I DON'T LIKE TO BRAG, BUT I'M PRETTY SMART.
IN CLASS, I CAN EXPLAIN PRACTICALLY ANYTHING! CHEMISTRY, PHYSICS, COMPUTERS...
SO WHY DID I JUST MAKE A COMPLETE FOOL OF MYSELF IN FRONT OF A GIRL I REALLY LIKE?
HOW CAN MATH BE SO EASY, BUT THIS SO HARD?
WHY CAN'T I GET MYSELF TOGETHER?
DO I COME ON TOO STRONG?
IS IT ME?
IT JUST FEELS LIKE MY LIFE IS DRAINING THROUGH MY HANDS AND I CAN'T HOLD ON!
I MEAN, AM I BETTER AT TALKING TO MACHINES THAN PEOPLE?

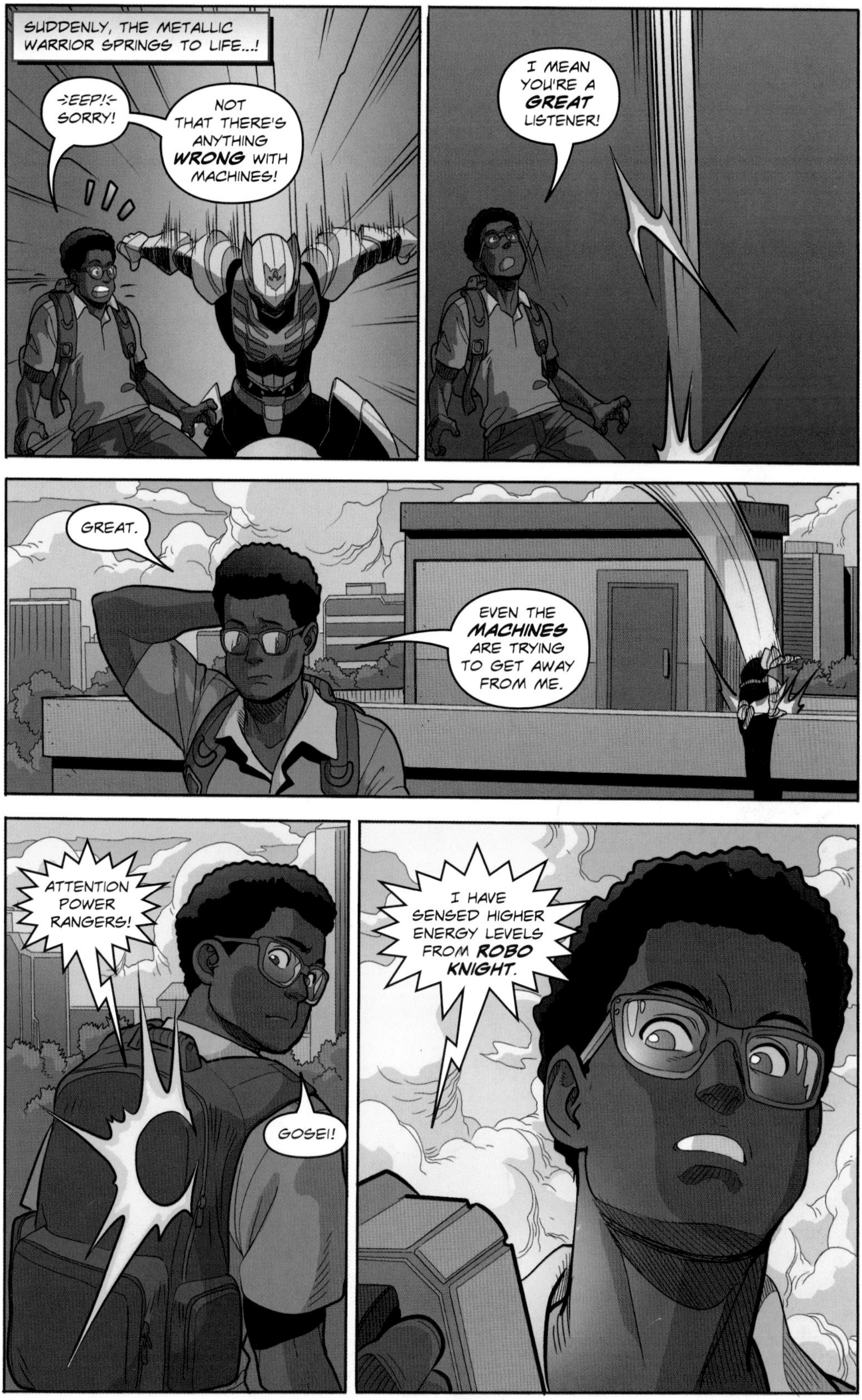
SUDDENLY, THE METALLIC WARRIOR SPRINGS TO LIFE...!
>EEP!< SORRY!
NOT THAT THERE'S ANYTHING WRONG WITH MACHINES!
I MEAN YOU'RE A GREAT LISTENER!
GREAT.
EVEN THE MACHINES ARE TRYING TO GET AWAY FROM ME.
ATTENTION POWER RANGERS!
GOSEI!
I HAVE SENSED HIGHER ENERGY LEVELS FROM ROBO KNIGHT.

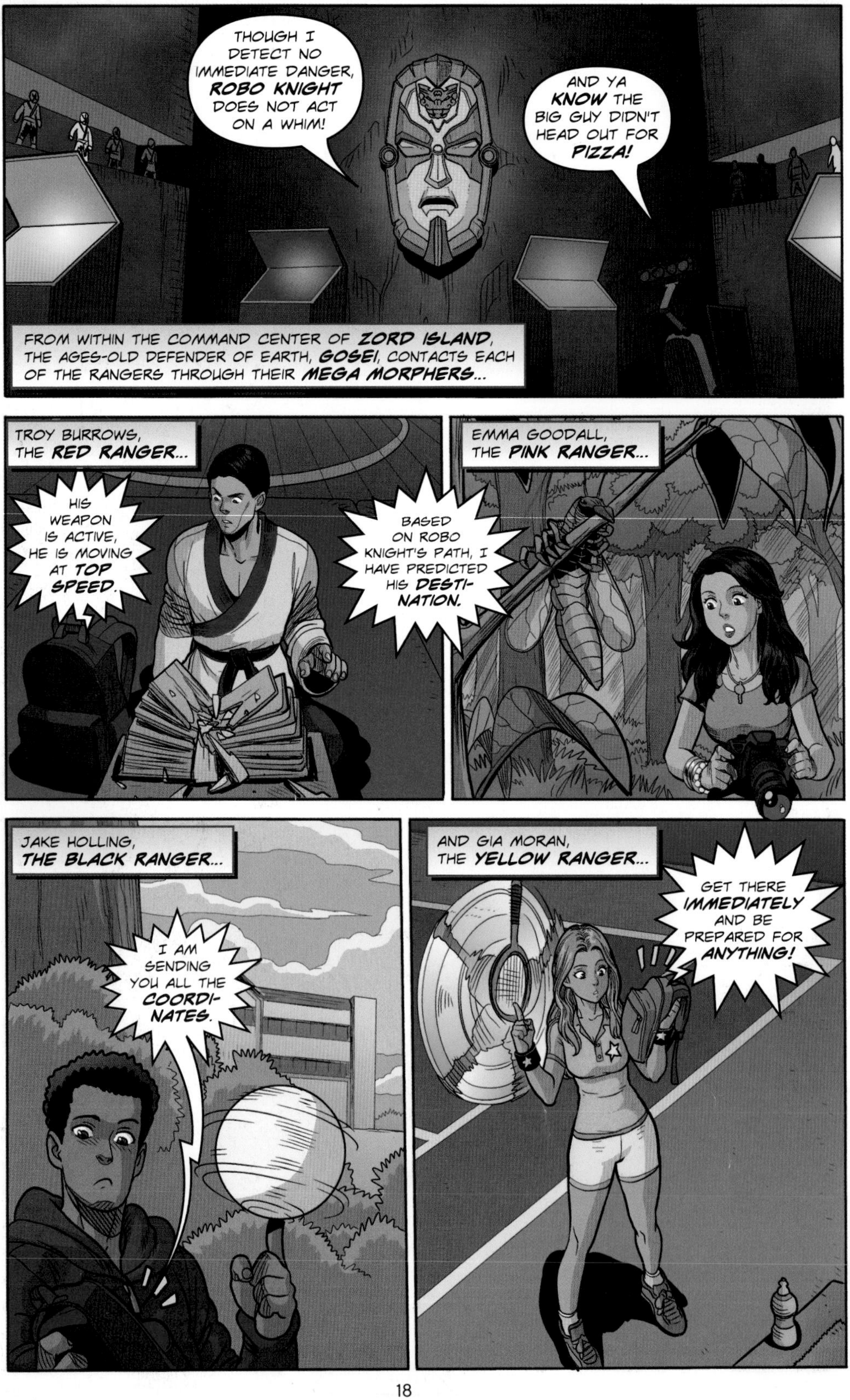

THOUGH I DETECT NO IMMEDIATE DANGER, ROBO KNIGHT DOES NOT ACT ON A WHIM!
AND YA KNOW THE BIG GUY DIDN'T HEAD OUT FOR PIZZA!
FROM WITHIN THE COMMAND CENTER OF ZORD ISLAND, THE AGES-OLD DEFENDER OF EARTH, GOSEI, CONTACTS EACH OF THE RANGERS THROUGH THEIR MEGA MORPHERS...
TROY BURROWS, THE RED RANGER...
HIS WEAPON IS ACTIVE, HE IS MOVING AT TOP SPEED.
EMMA GOODALL, THE PINK RANGER...
BASED ON ROBO KNIGHT'S PATH, I HAVE PREDICTED HIS DESTI-NATION.
JAKE HOLLING, THE BLACK RANGER...
I AM SENDING YOU ALL THE COORDI-NATES.
AND GIA MORAN, THE YELLOW RANGER...
GET THERE IMMEDIATELY AND BE PREPARED FOR ANYTHING!

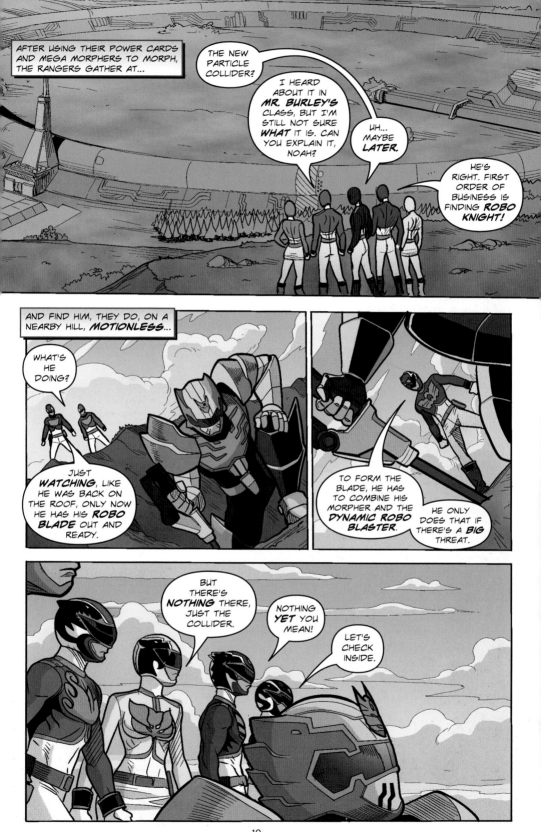

AFTER USING THEIR POWER CARDS AND MEGA MORPHERS TO MORPH, THE RANGERS GATHER AT...

THE NEW PARTICLE COLLIDER?

I HEARD ABOUT IT IN **MR. BURLEY'S** CLASS, BUT I'M STILL NOT SURE **WHAT** IT IS. CAN YOU EXPLAIN IT, NOAH?

UH... MAYBE **LATER.**

HE'S RIGHT. FIRST ORDER OF BUSINESS IS FINDING **ROBO KNIGHT!**

AND FIND HIM, THEY DO, ON A NEARBY HILL, **MOTIONLESS...**

WHAT'S HE DOING?

JUST **WATCHING**, LIKE HE WAS BACK ON THE ROOF, ONLY NOW HE HAS HIS **ROBO BLADE** OUT AND READY.

TO FORM THE BLADE, HE HAS TO COMBINE HIS MORPHER AND THE **DYNAMIC ROBO BLASTER.**

HE ONLY DOES THAT IF THERE'S A **BIG** THREAT.

BUT THERE'S **NOTHING** THERE, JUST THE COLLIDER.

NOTHING **YET** YOU MEAN!

LET'S CHECK INSIDE.

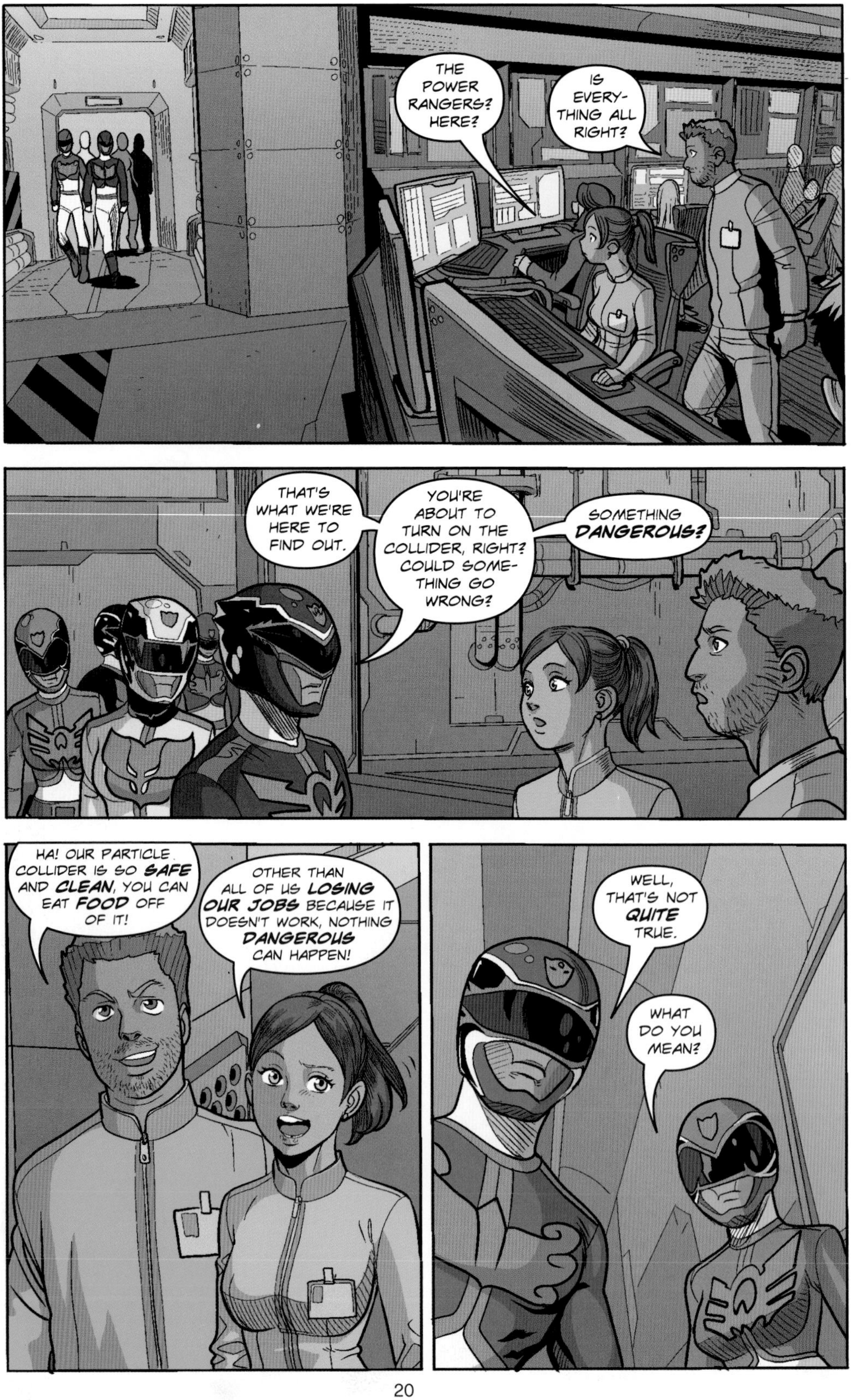
THE POWER RANGERS? HERE?
IS EVERY-THING ALL RIGHT?
THAT'S WHAT WE'RE HERE TO FIND OUT.
YOU'RE ABOUT TO TURN ON THE COLLIDER, RIGHT? COULD SOME-THING GO WRONG?
SOMETHING DANGEROUS?
HA! OUR PARTICLE COLLIDER IS SO SAFE AND CLEAN, YOU CAN EAT FOOD OFF OF IT!
OTHER THAN ALL OF US LOSING OUR JOBS BECAUSE IT DOESN'T WORK, NOTHING DANGEROUS CAN HAPPEN!
WELL, THAT'S NOT QUITE TRUE.
WHAT DO YOU MEAN?

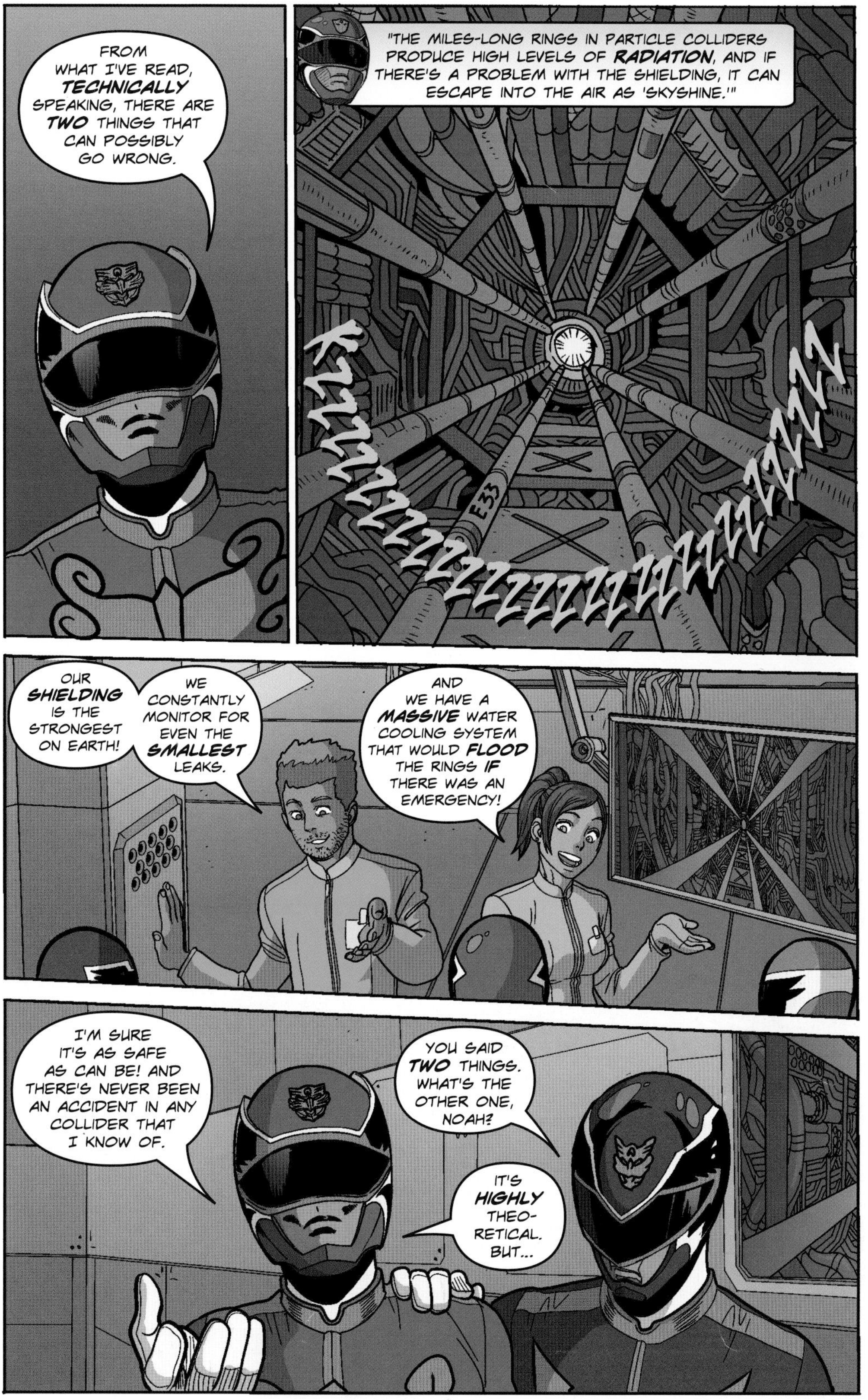
FROM WHAT I'VE READ, TECHNICALLY SPEAKING, THERE ARE TWO THINGS THAT CAN POSSIBLY GO WRONG.
"THE MILES-LONG RINGS IN PARTICLE COLLIDERS PRODUCE HIGH LEVELS OF RADIATION, AND IF THERE'S A PROBLEM WITH THE SHIELDING, IT CAN ESCAPE INTO THE AIR AS 'SKYSHINE.'"
KZZZZZZZZZZZZZZZZZZZZZZZZZZZZZZZZZ
E33
OUR SHIELDING IS THE STRONGEST ON EARTH!
WE CONSTANTLY MONITOR FOR EVEN THE SMALLEST LEAKS.
AND WE HAVE A MASSIVE WATER COOLING SYSTEM THAT WOULD FLOOD THE RINGS IF THERE WAS AN EMERGENCY!
I'M SURE IT'S AS SAFE AS CAN BE! AND THERE'S NEVER BEEN AN ACCIDENT IN ANY COLLIDER THAT I KNOW OF.
YOU SAID TWO THINGS. WHAT'S THE OTHER ONE, NOAH?
IT'S HIGHLY THEO-RETICAL. BUT...

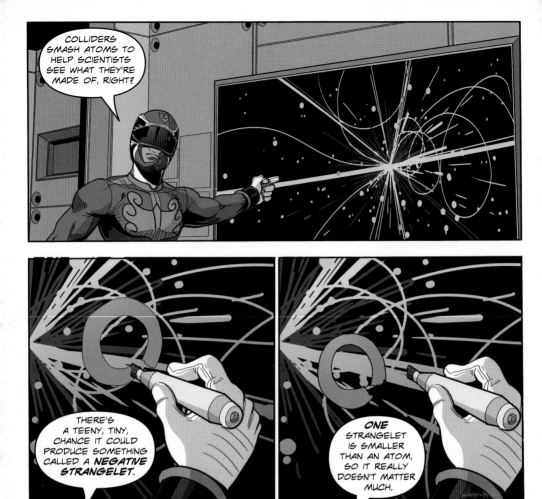

COLLIDERS SMASH ATOMS TO HELP SCIENTISTS SEE WHAT THEY'RE MADE OF, RIGHT?

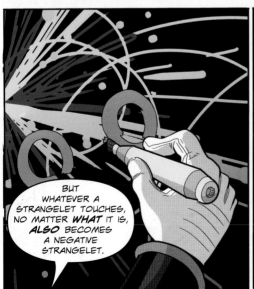

THERE'S A TEENY, TINY, CHANCE IT COULD PRODUCE SOMETHING CALLED A *NEGATIVE STRANGELET.*

ONE STRANGELET IS SMALLER THAN AN ATOM, SO IT REALLY DOESN'T MATTER MUCH.

BUT WHATEVER A STRANGELET TOUCHES, NO MATTER *WHAT* IT IS, *ALSO* BECOMES A NEGATIVE STRANGELET.

WHEN *TWO* STRANGELETS HIT SOMETHING, THEY MAKE *FOUR.*

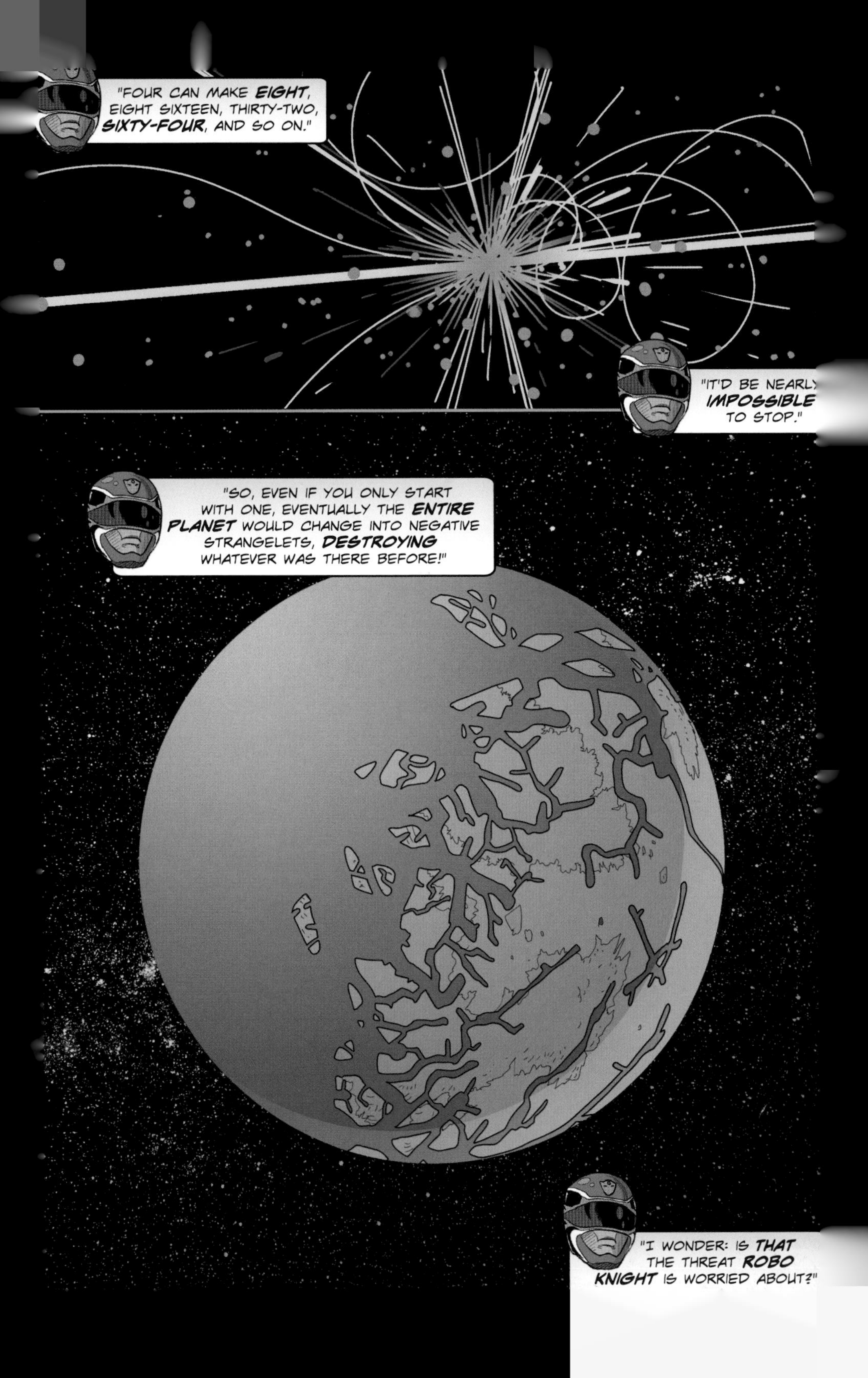
"FOUR CAN MAKE EIGHT, EIGHT SIXTEEN, THIRTY-TWO, SIXTY-FOUR, AND SO ON."
"IT'D BE NEARLY IMPOSSIBLE TO STOP."
"SO, EVEN IF YOU ONLY START WITH ONE, EVENTUALLY THE ENTIRE PLANET WOULD CHANGE INTO NEGATIVE STRANGELETS, DESTROYING WHATEVER WAS THERE BEFORE!"
"I WONDER: IS THAT THE THREAT ROBO KNIGHT IS WORRIED ABOUT?"

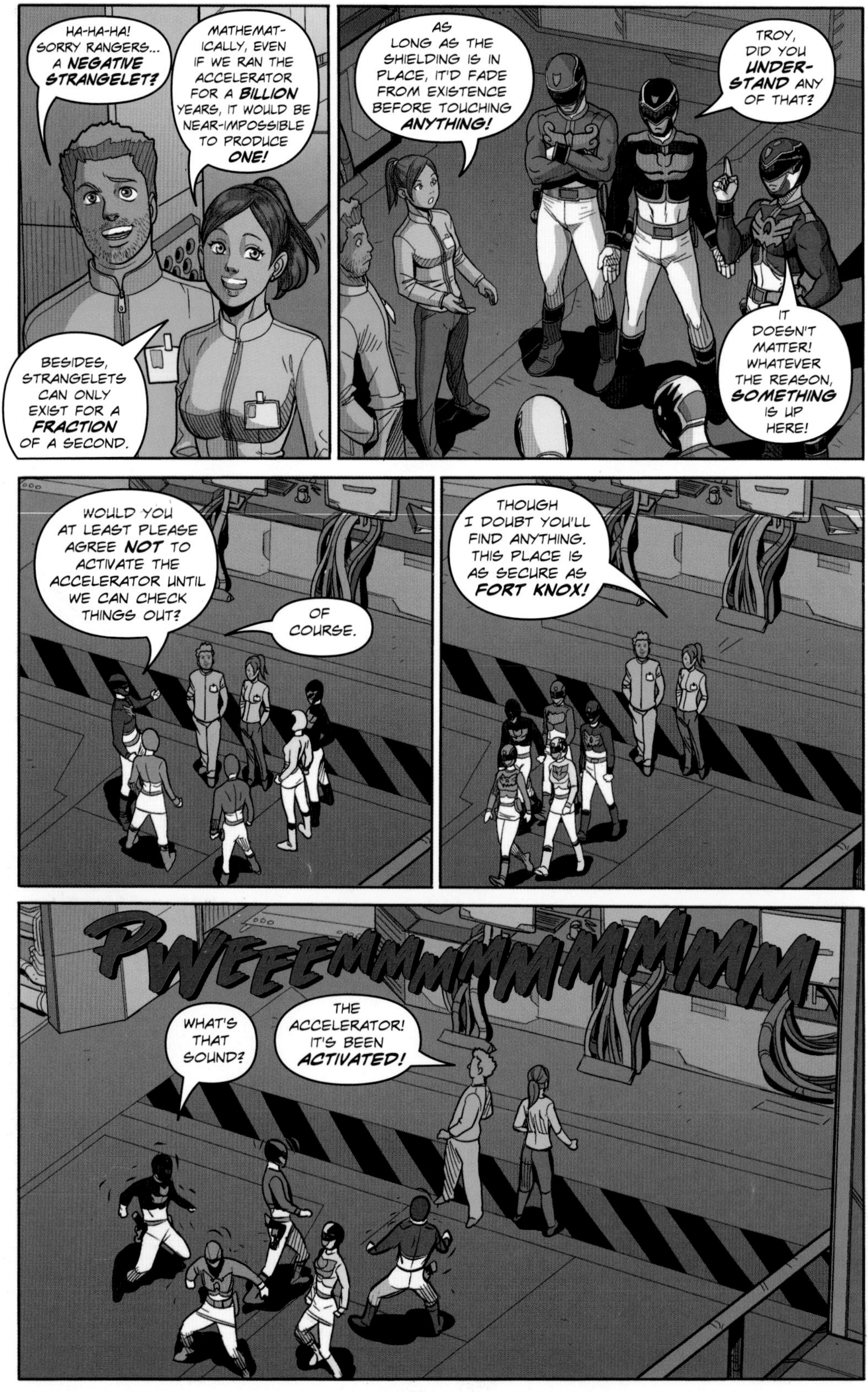
HA-HA-HA! SORRY RANGERS... A NEGATIVE STRANGELET?
MATHEMATICALLY, EVEN IF WE RAN THE ACCELERATOR FOR A BILLION YEARS, IT WOULD BE NEAR-IMPOSSIBLE TO PRODUCE ONE!
BESIDES, STRANGELETS CAN ONLY EXIST FOR A FRACTION OF A SECOND.
AS LONG AS THE SHIELDING IS IN PLACE, IT'D FADE FROM EXISTENCE BEFORE TOUCHING ANYTHING!
TROY, DID YOU UNDERSTAND ANY OF THAT?
IT DOESN'T MATTER! WHATEVER THE REASON, SOMETHING IS UP HERE!
WOULD YOU AT LEAST PLEASE AGREE NOT TO ACTIVATE THE ACCELERATOR UNTIL WE CAN CHECK THINGS OUT?
OF COURSE.
THOUGH I DOUBT YOU'LL FIND ANYTHING. THIS PLACE IS AS SECURE AS FORT KNOX!
PWEEEMMMMMMMMMMM
WHAT'S THAT SOUND?
THE ACCELERATOR! IT'S BEEN ACTIVATED!

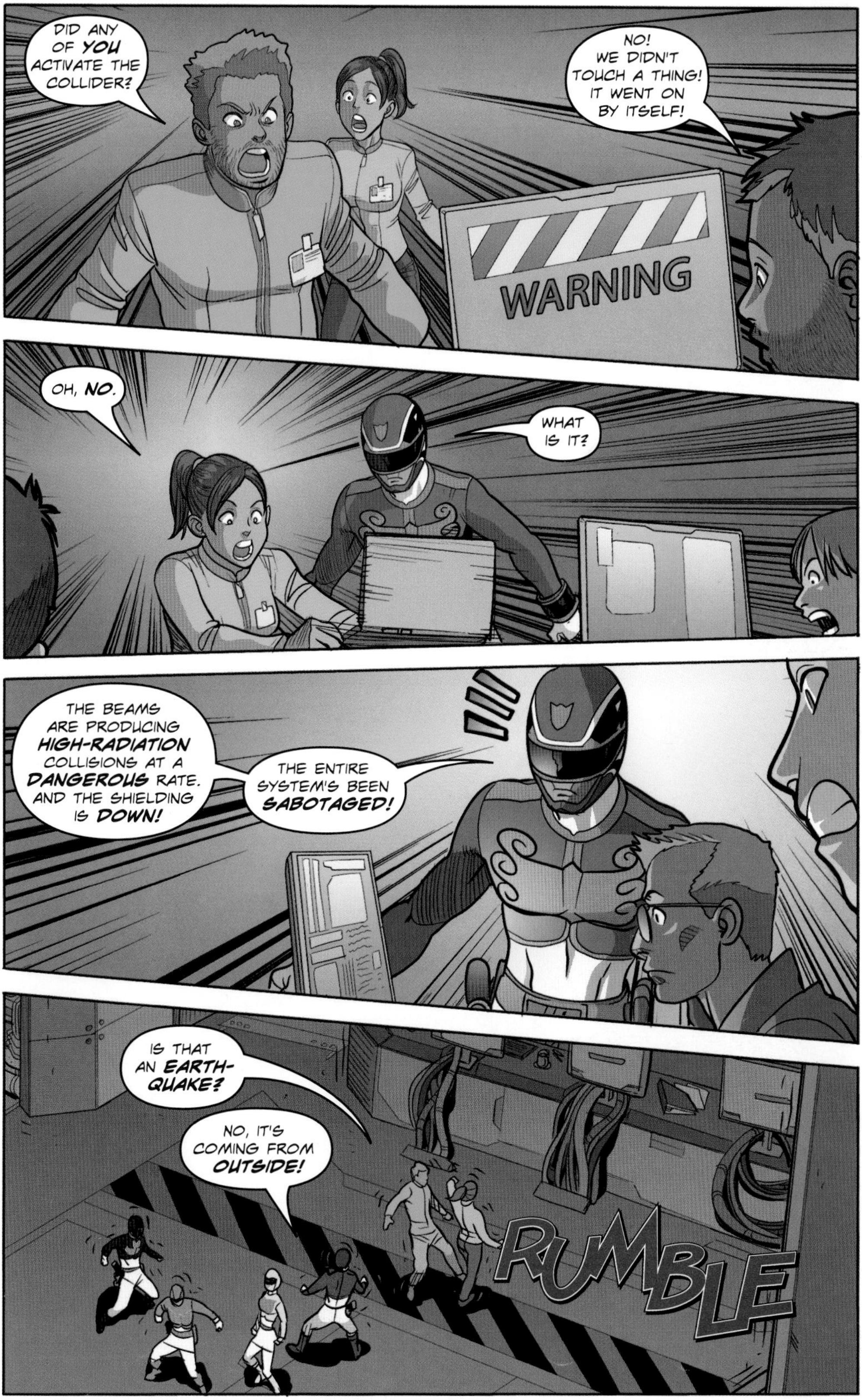
DID ANY OF YOU ACTIVATE THE COLLIDER?
NO! WE DIDN'T TOUCH A THING! IT WENT ON BY ITSELF!
WARNING
OH, NO.
WHAT IS IT?
THE BEAMS ARE PRODUCING HIGH-RADIATION COLLISIONS AT A DANGEROUS RATE. AND THE SHIELDING IS DOWN!
THE ENTIRE SYSTEM'S BEEN SABOTAGED!
IS THAT AN EARTH-QUAKE?
NO, IT'S COMING FROM OUTSIDE!
RUMBLE

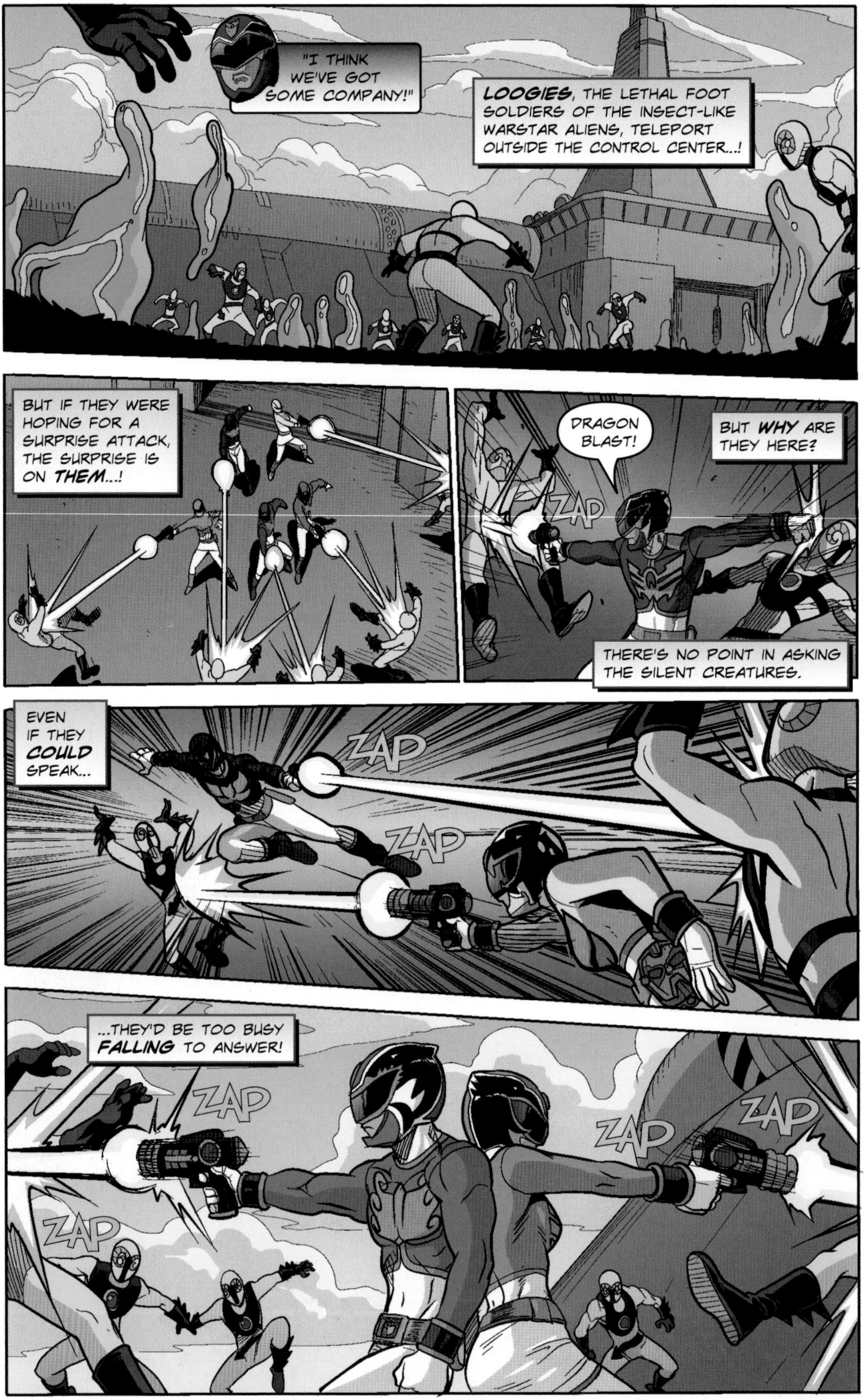
"I THINK WE'VE GOT SOME COMPANY!"
LOOGIES, THE LETHAL FOOT SOLDIERS OF THE INSECT-LIKE WARSTAR ALIENS, TELEPORT OUTSIDE THE CONTROL CENTER...!
BUT IF THEY WERE HOPING FOR A SURPRISE ATTACK, THE SURPRISE IS ON **THEM**...!
DRAGON BLAST!
ZAP
BUT **WHY** ARE THEY HERE?
THERE'S NO POINT IN ASKING THE SILENT CREATURES.
EVEN IF THEY **COULD** SPEAK...
ZAP
ZAP
...THEY'D BE TOO BUSY **FALLING** TO ANSWER!
ZAP
ZAP
ZAP
ZAP

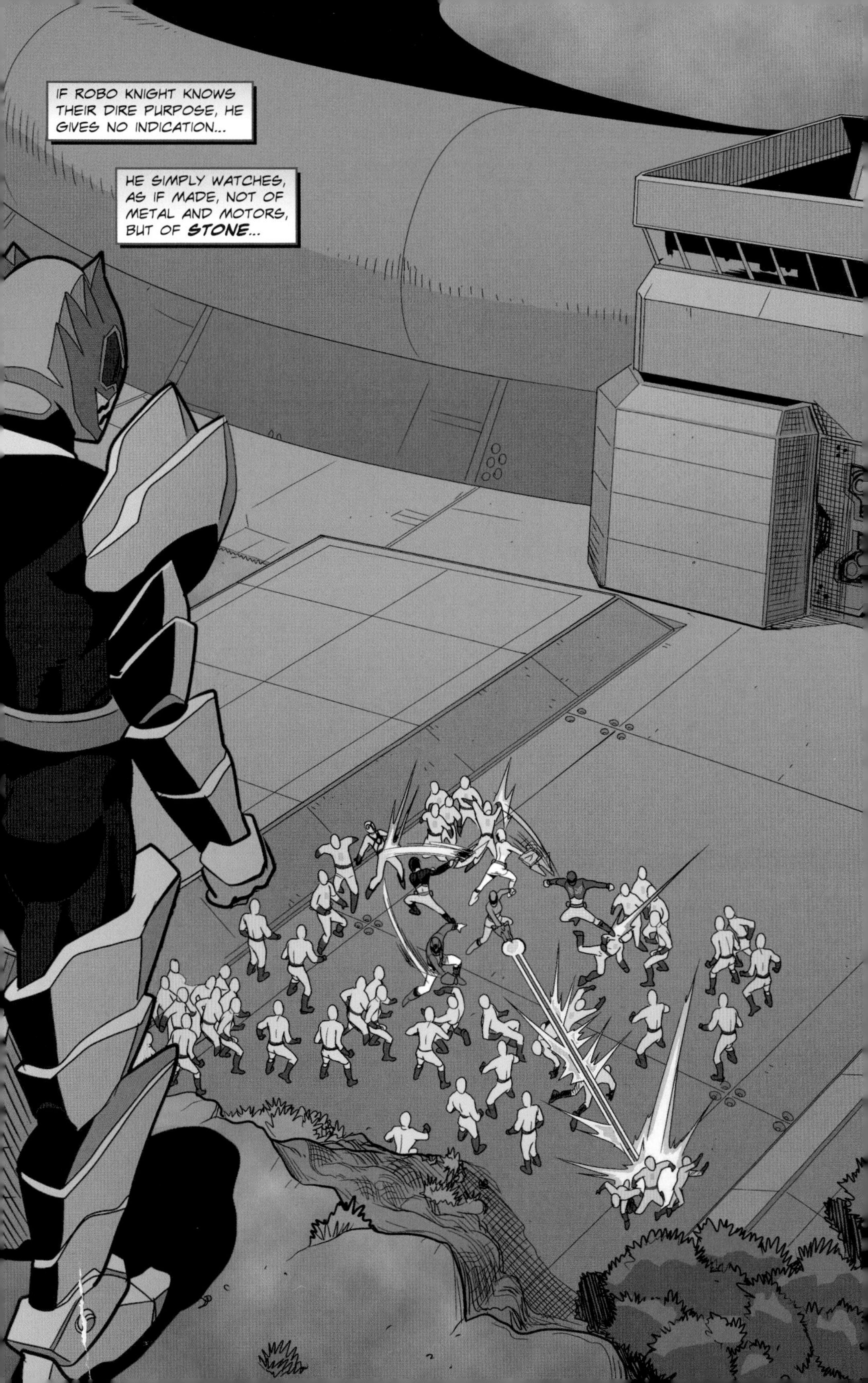
IF ROBO KNIGHT KNOWS THEIR DIRE PURPOSE, HE GIVES NO INDICATION...
HE SIMPLY WATCHES, AS IF MADE, NOT OF METAL AND MOTORS, BUT OF STONE...

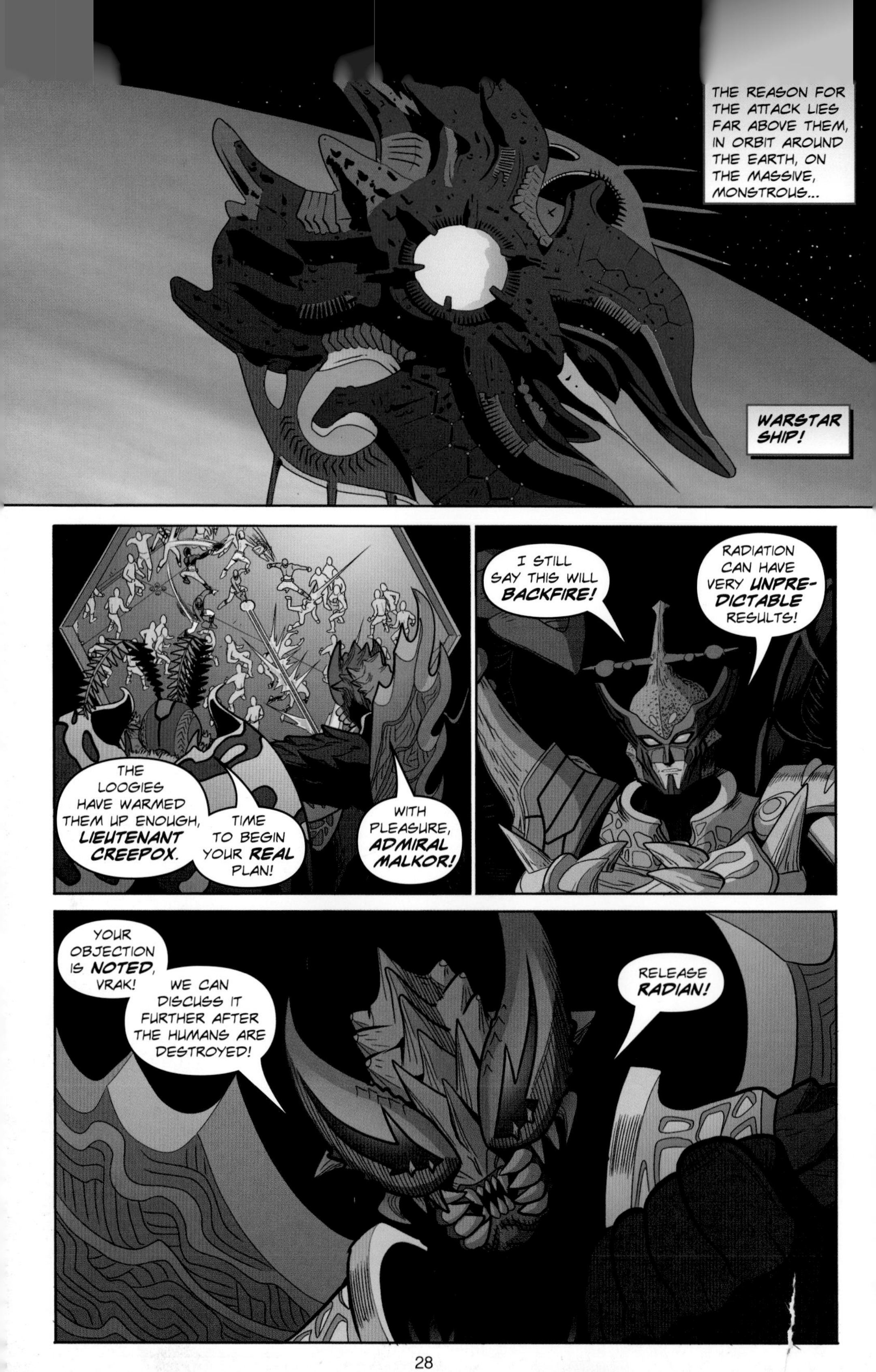
THE REASON FOR THE ATTACK LIES FAR ABOVE THEM, IN ORBIT AROUND THE EARTH, ON THE MASSIVE, MONSTROUS...
WARSTAR SHIP!
THE LOOGIES HAVE WARMED THEM UP ENOUGH, LIEUTENANT CREEPOX.
TIME TO BEGIN YOUR REAL PLAN!
WITH PLEASURE, ADMIRAL MALKOR!
I STILL SAY THIS WILL BACKFIRE!
RADIATION CAN HAVE VERY UNPREDICTABLE RESULTS!
YOUR OBJECTION IS NOTED, VRAK!
WE CAN DISCUSS IT FURTHER AFTER THE HUMANS ARE DESTROYED!
RELEASE RADIAN!

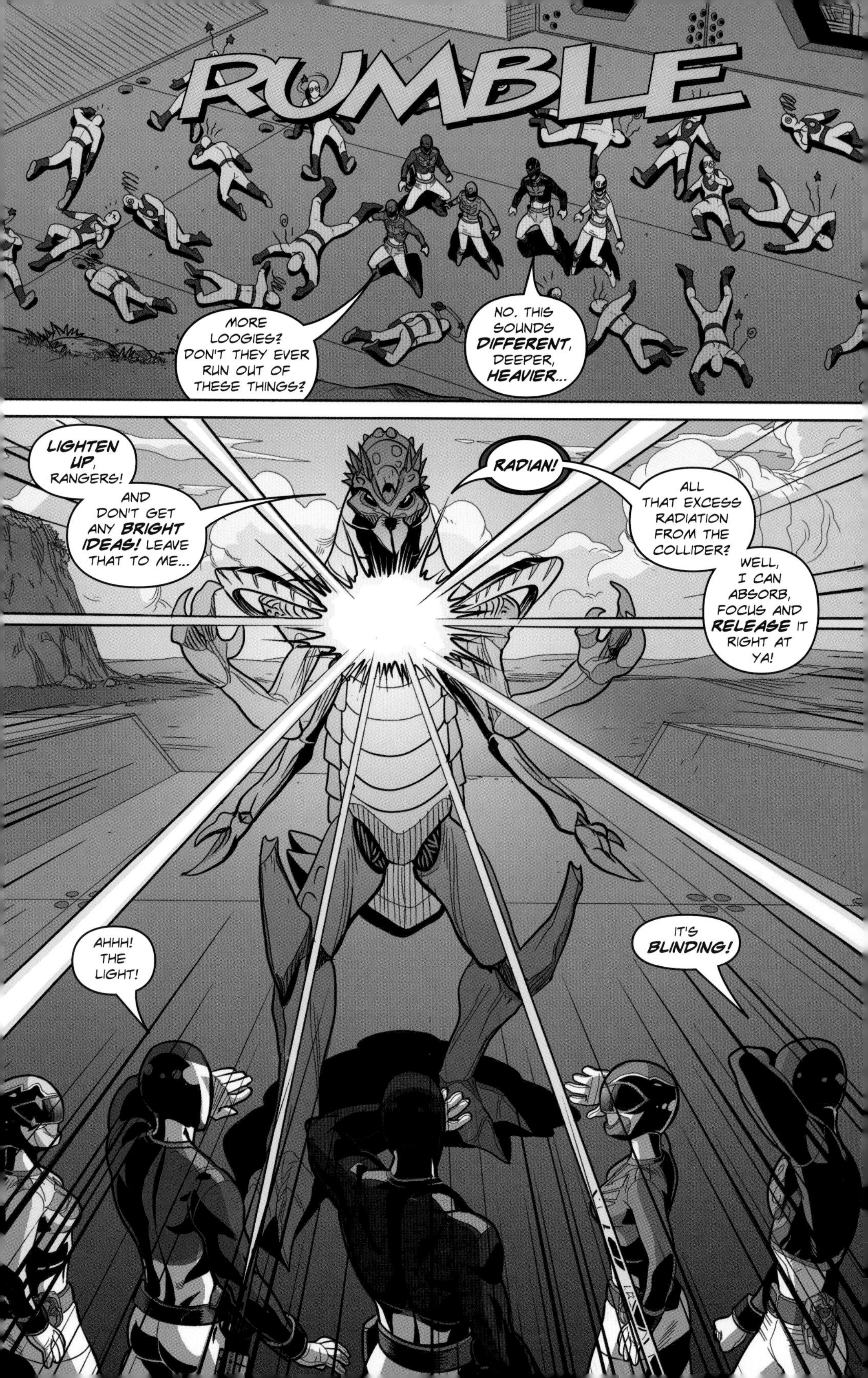
RUMBLE
MORE LOOGIES? DON'T THEY EVER RUN OUT OF THESE THINGS?
NO. THIS SOUNDS DIFFERENT, DEEPER, HEAVIER...
LIGHTEN UP, RANGERS!
AND DON'T GET ANY BRIGHT IDEAS! LEAVE THAT TO ME...
RADIAN!
ALL THAT EXCESS RADIATION FROM THE COLLIDER?
WELL, I CAN ABSORB, FOCUS AND RELEASE IT RIGHT AT YA!
AHHH! THE LIGHT!
IT'S BLINDING!

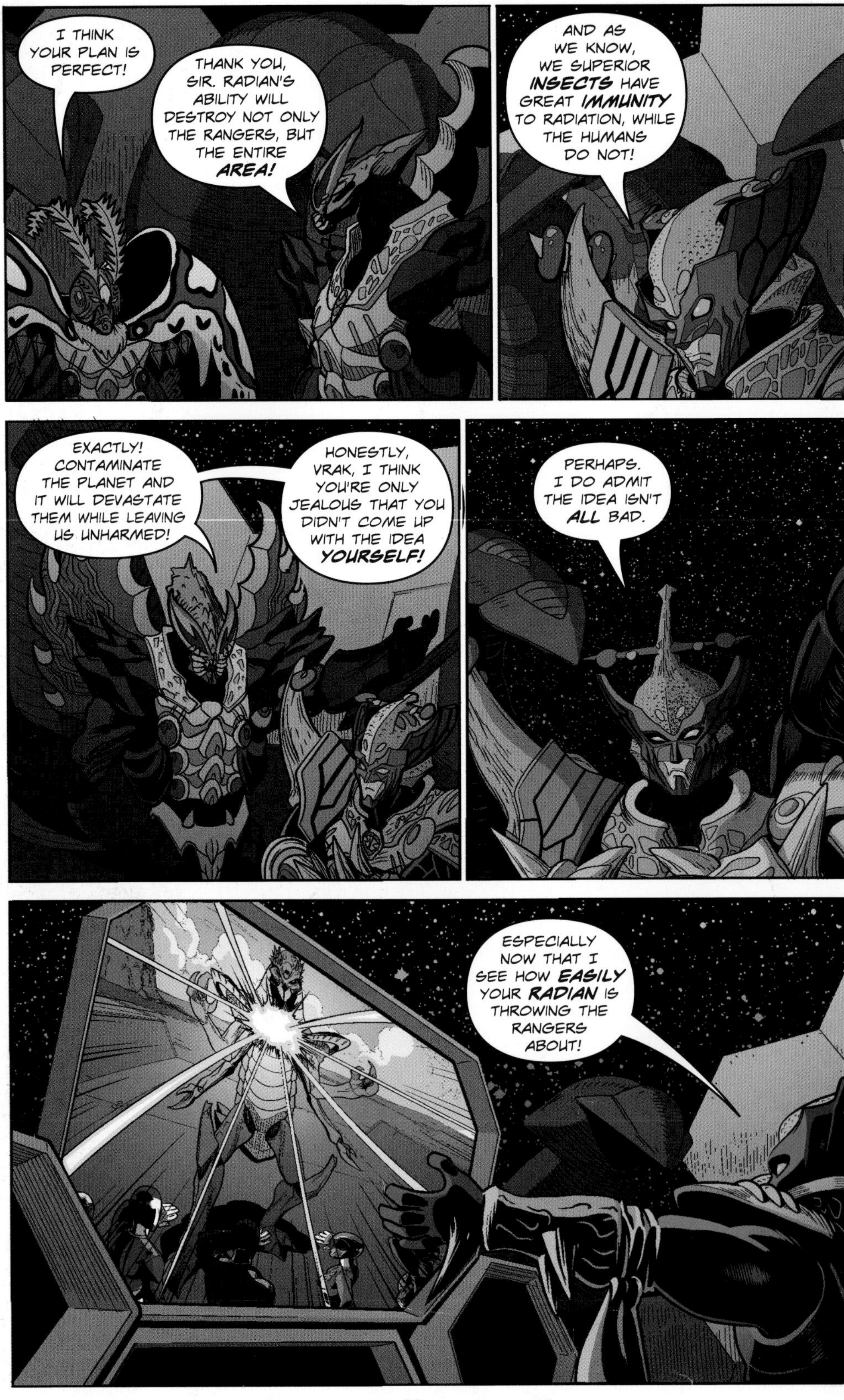
I THINK YOUR PLAN IS PERFECT!
THANK YOU, SIR. RADIAN'S ABILITY WILL DESTROY NOT ONLY THE RANGERS, BUT THE ENTIRE **AREA!**
AND AS WE KNOW, WE SUPERIOR **INSECTS** HAVE GREAT **IMMUNITY** TO RADIATION, WHILE THE HUMANS DO NOT!
EXACTLY! CONTAMINATE THE PLANET AND IT WILL DEVASTATE THEM WHILE LEAVING US UNHARMED!
HONESTLY, VRAK, I THINK YOU'RE ONLY JEALOUS THAT YOU DIDN'T COME UP WITH THE IDEA **YOURSELF!**
PERHAPS. I DO ADMIT THE IDEA ISN'T **ALL** BAD.
ESPECIALLY NOW THAT I SEE HOW **EASILY** YOUR **RADIAN** IS THROWING THE RANGERS ABOUT!

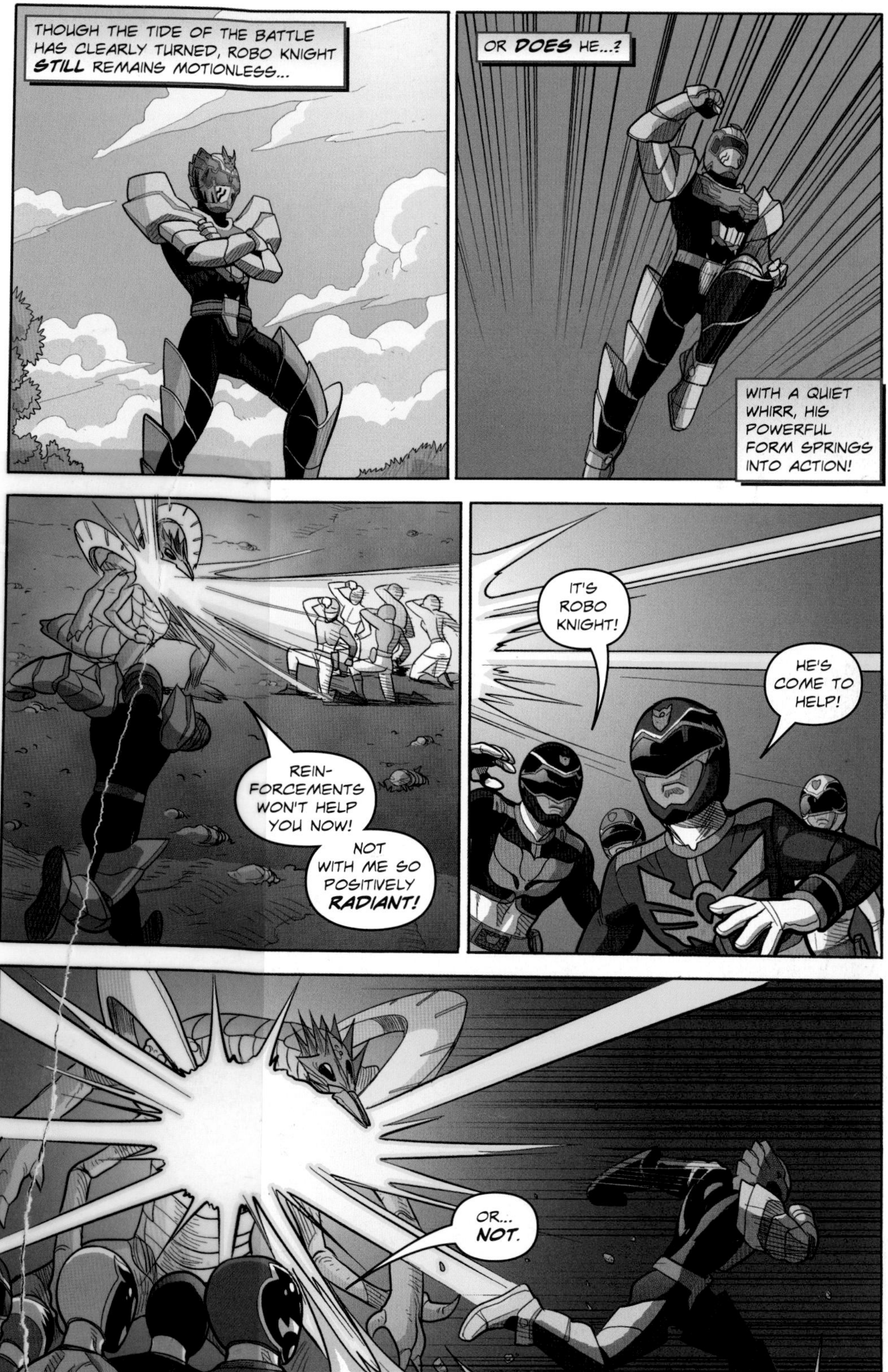
THOUGH THE TIDE OF THE BATTLE HAS CLEARLY TURNED, ROBO KNIGHT STILL REMAINS MOTIONLESS...
OR DOES HE...?
WITH A QUIET WHIRR, HIS POWERFUL FORM SPRINGS INTO ACTION!
REIN-FORCEMENTS WON'T HELP YOU NOW!
NOT WITH ME SO POSITIVELY RADIANT!
IT'S ROBO KNIGHT!
HE'S COME TO HELP!
OR... NOT.

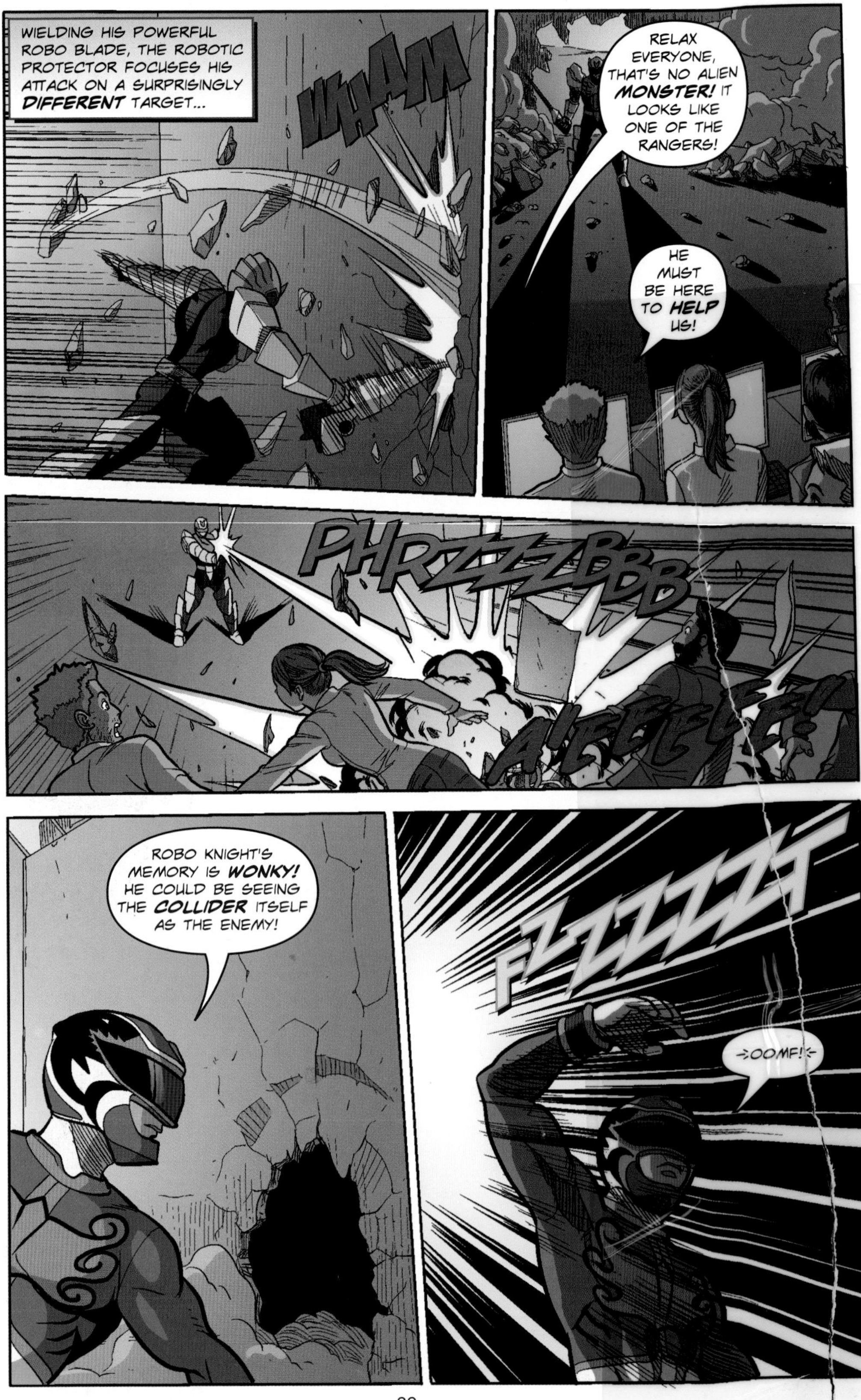
WIELDING HIS POWERFUL ROBO BLADE, THE ROBOTIC PROTECTOR FOCUSES HIS ATTACK ON A SURPRISINGLY DIFFERENT TARGET...
WHAM
RELAX EVERYONE, THAT'S NO ALIEN MONSTER! IT LOOKS LIKE ONE OF THE RANGERS!
HE MUST BE HERE TO HELP US!
PHRZZZZBBB
A'EEEEEE!
ROBO KNIGHT'S MEMORY IS WONKY! HE COULD BE SEEING THE COLLIDER ITSELF AS THE ENEMY!
FZZZZZT
OOMF!

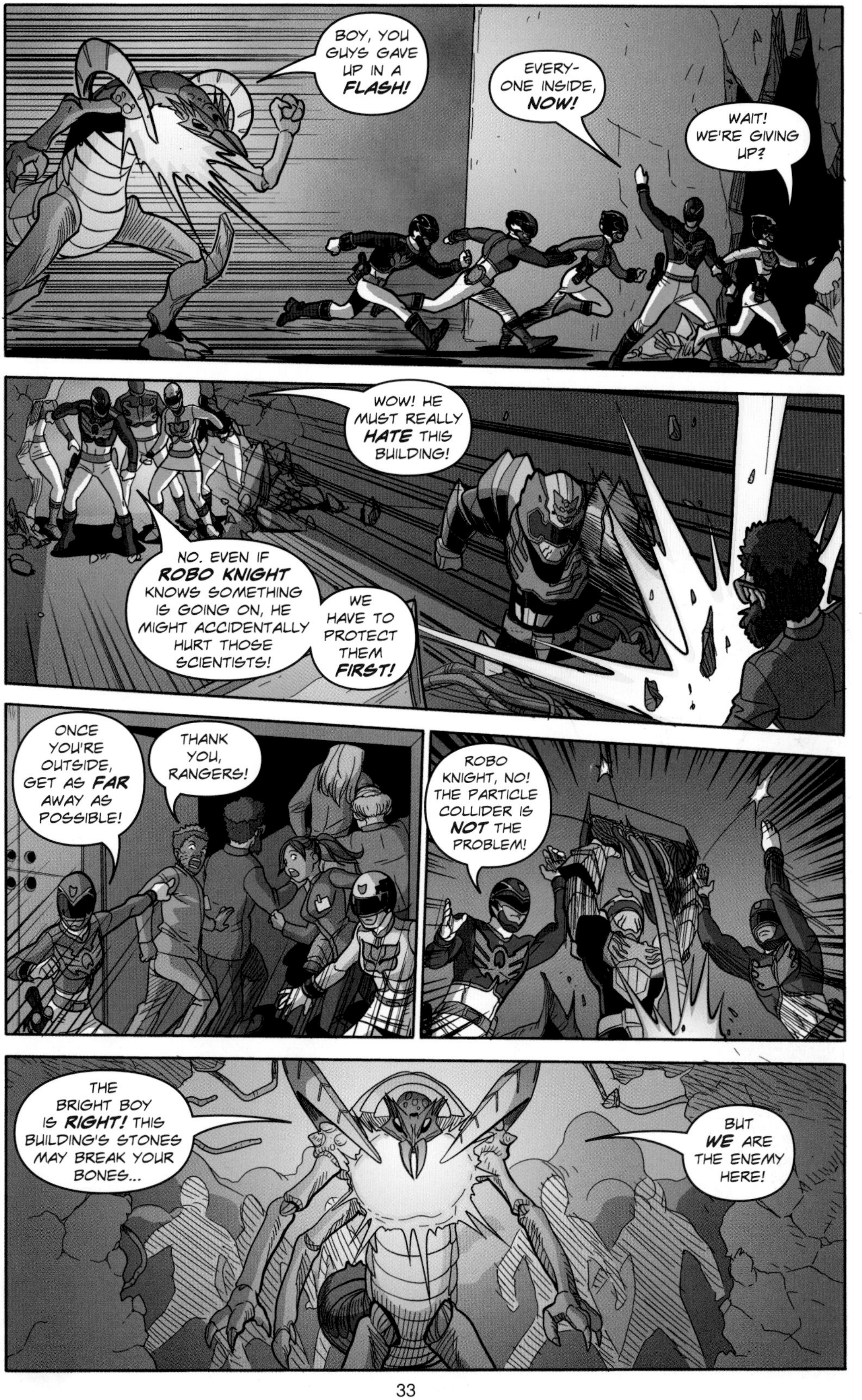
BOY, YOU GUYS GAVE UP IN A FLASH!
EVERY-ONE INSIDE, NOW!
WAIT! WE'RE GIVING UP?
WOW! HE MUST REALLY HATE THIS BUILDING!
NO. EVEN IF ROBO KNIGHT KNOWS SOMETHING IS GOING ON, HE MIGHT ACCIDENTALLY HURT THOSE SCIENTISTS!
WE HAVE TO PROTECT THEM FIRST!
ONCE YOU'RE OUTSIDE, GET AS FAR AWAY AS POSSIBLE!
THANK YOU, RANGERS!
ROBO KNIGHT, NO! THE PARTICLE COLLIDER IS NOT THE PROBLEM!
THE BRIGHT BOY IS RIGHT! THIS BUILDING'S STONES MAY BREAK YOUR BONES...
BUT WE ARE THE ENEMY HERE!

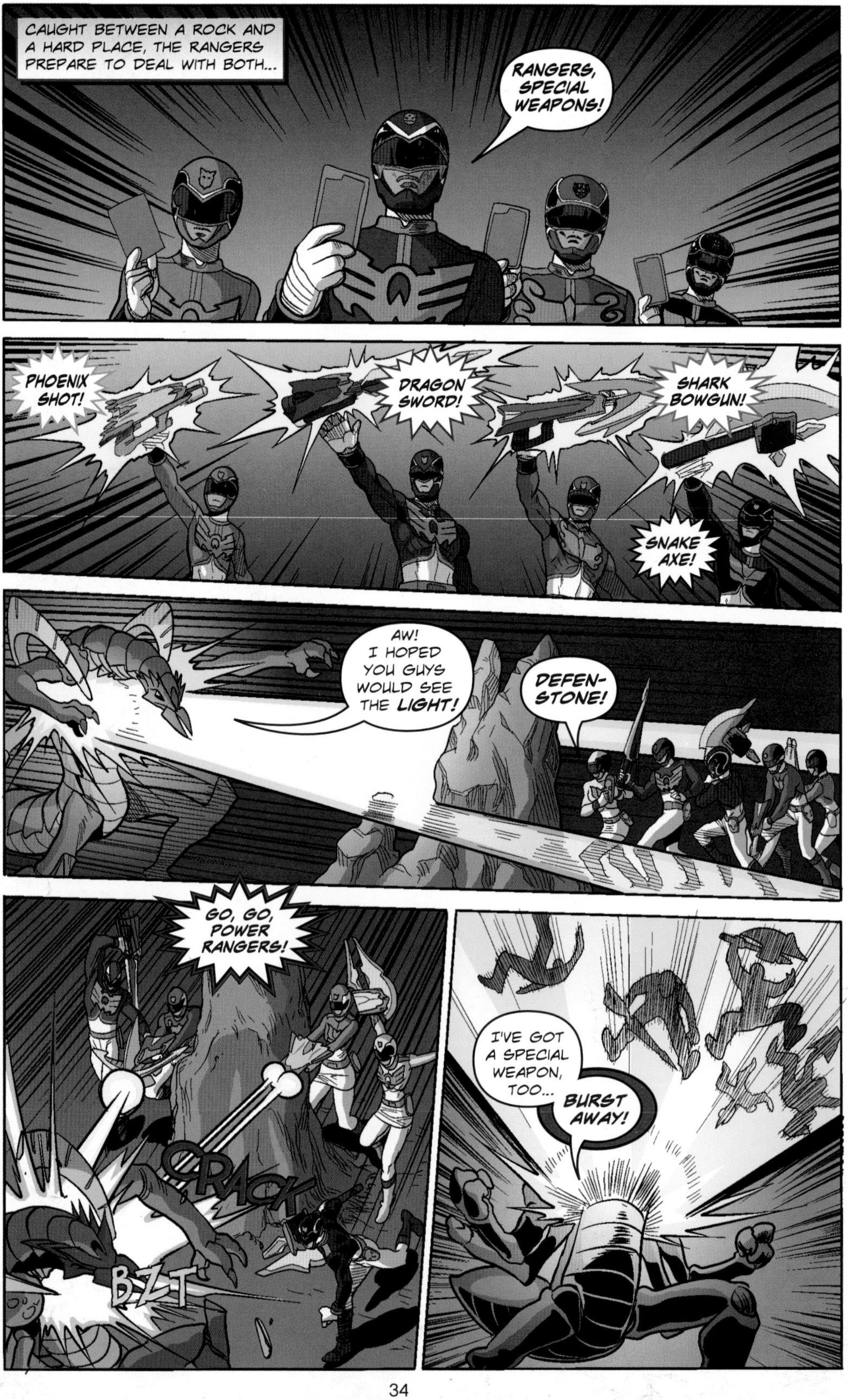
CAUGHT BETWEEN A ROCK AND A HARD PLACE, THE RANGERS PREPARE TO DEAL WITH BOTH...
RANGERS, SPECIAL WEAPONS!
PHOENIX SHOT!
DRAGON SWORD!
SHARK BOWGUN!
SNAKE AXE!
AW! I HOPED YOU GUYS WOULD SEE THE LIGHT!
DEFEN-STONE!
GO, GO, POWER RANGERS!
CRACK
BZZT
I'VE GOT A SPECIAL WEAPON, TOO...
BURST AWAY!

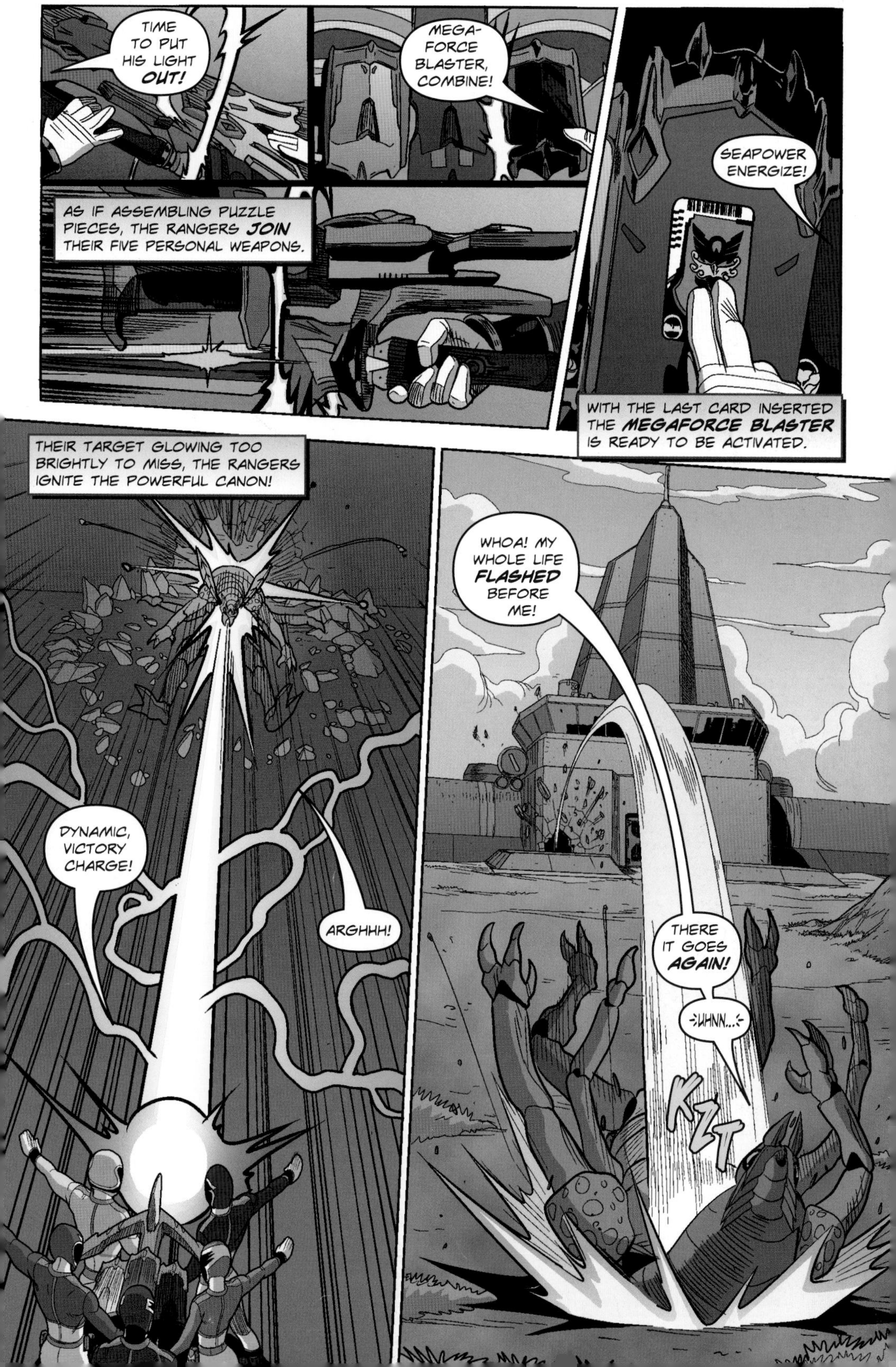
TIME TO PUT HIS LIGHT OUT!
MEGA-FORCE BLASTER, COMBINE!
SEAPOWER ENERGIZE!
AS IF ASSEMBLING PUZZLE PIECES, THE RANGERS JOIN THEIR FIVE PERSONAL WEAPONS.
WITH THE LAST CARD INSERTED THE MEGAFORCE BLASTER IS READY TO BE ACTIVATED.
THEIR TARGET GLOWING TOO BRIGHTLY TO MISS, THE RANGERS IGNITE THE POWERFUL CANON!
DYNAMIC, VICTORY CHARGE!
ARGHHH!
WHOA! MY WHOLE LIFE FLASHED BEFORE ME!
THERE IT GOES AGAIN!
UHNN...
KZT

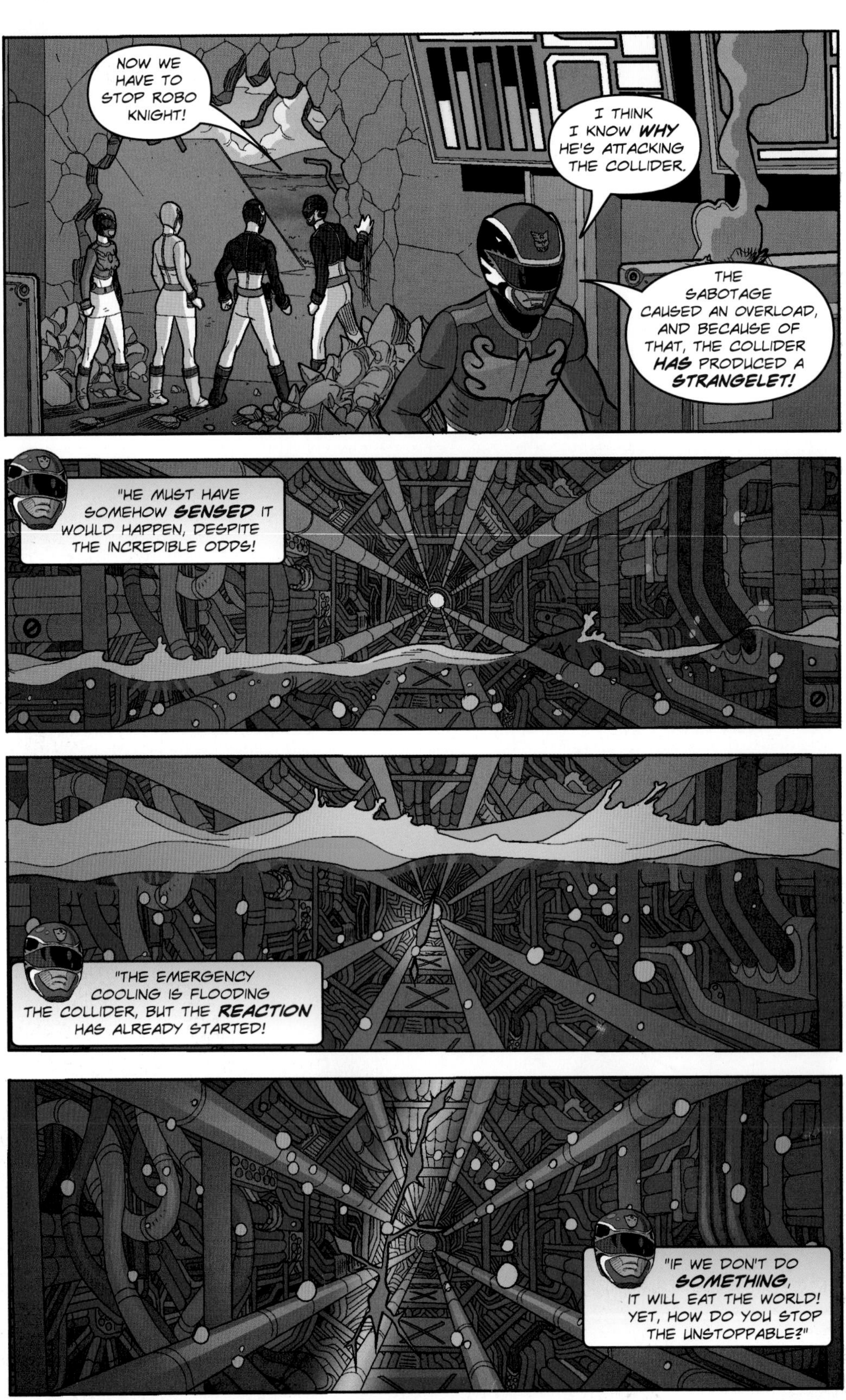
NOW WE HAVE TO STOP ROBO KNIGHT!
I THINK I KNOW WHY HE'S ATTACKING THE COLLIDER.
THE SABOTAGE CAUSED AN OVERLOAD, AND BECAUSE OF THAT, THE COLLIDER HAS PRODUCED A STRANGELET!
"HE MUST HAVE SOMEHOW SENSED IT WOULD HAPPEN, DESPITE THE INCREDIBLE ODDS!
"THE EMERGENCY COOLING IS FLOODING THE COLLIDER, BUT THE REACTION HAS ALREADY STARTED!
"IF WE DON'T DO SOMETHING, IT WILL EAT THE WORLD! YET, HOW DO YOU STOP THE UNSTOPPABLE?"

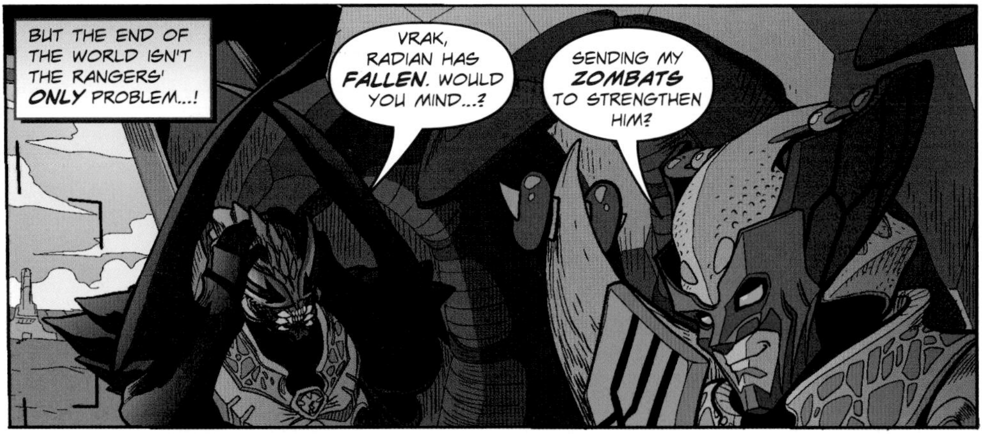
BUT THE END OF THE WORLD ISN'T THE RANGERS' ONLY PROBLEM...!
VRAK, RADIAN HAS FALLEN. WOULD YOU MIND...?
SENDING MY ZOMBATS TO STRENGTHEN HIM?

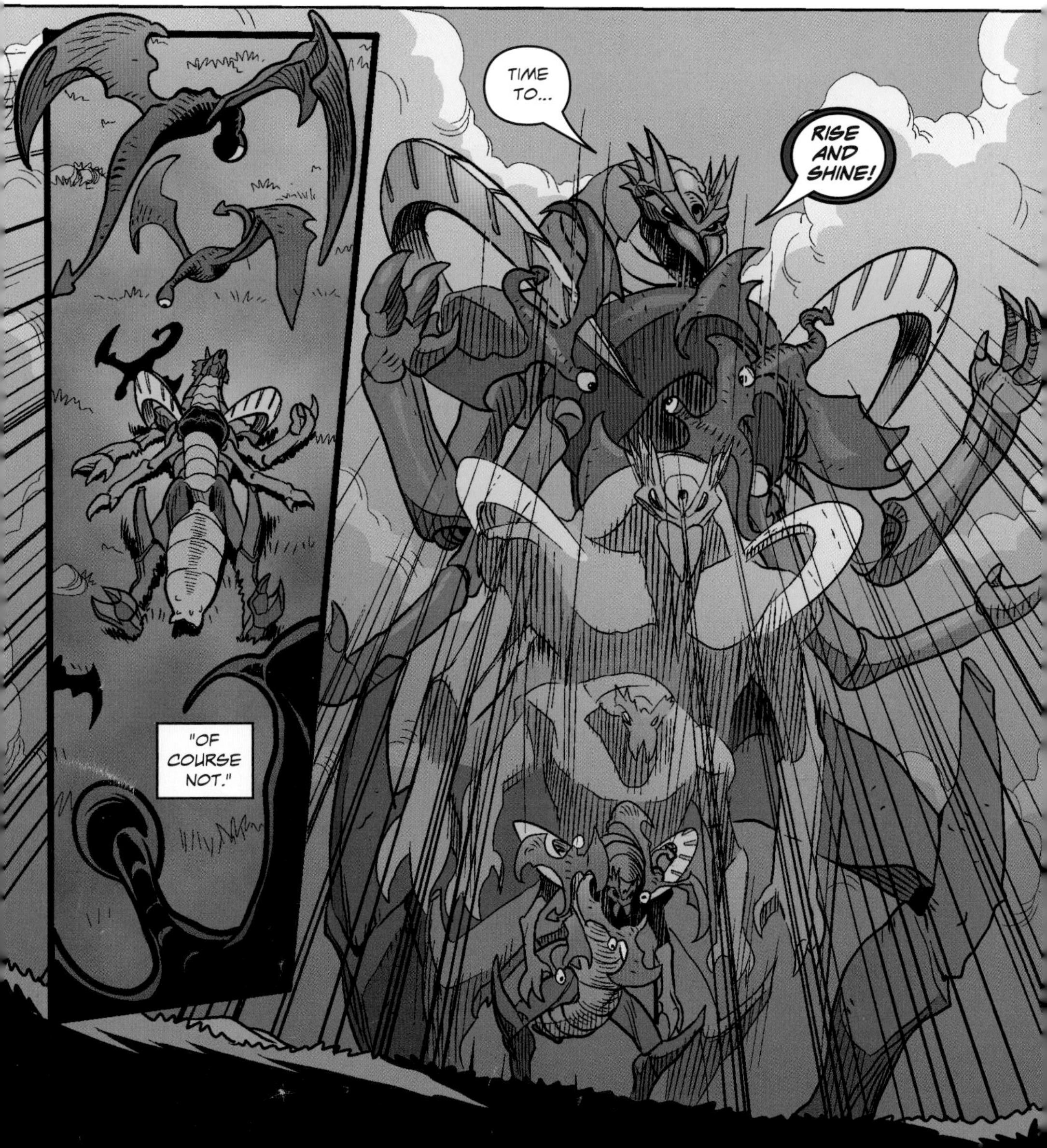
"OF COURSE NOT."
TIME TO...
RISE AND SHINE!

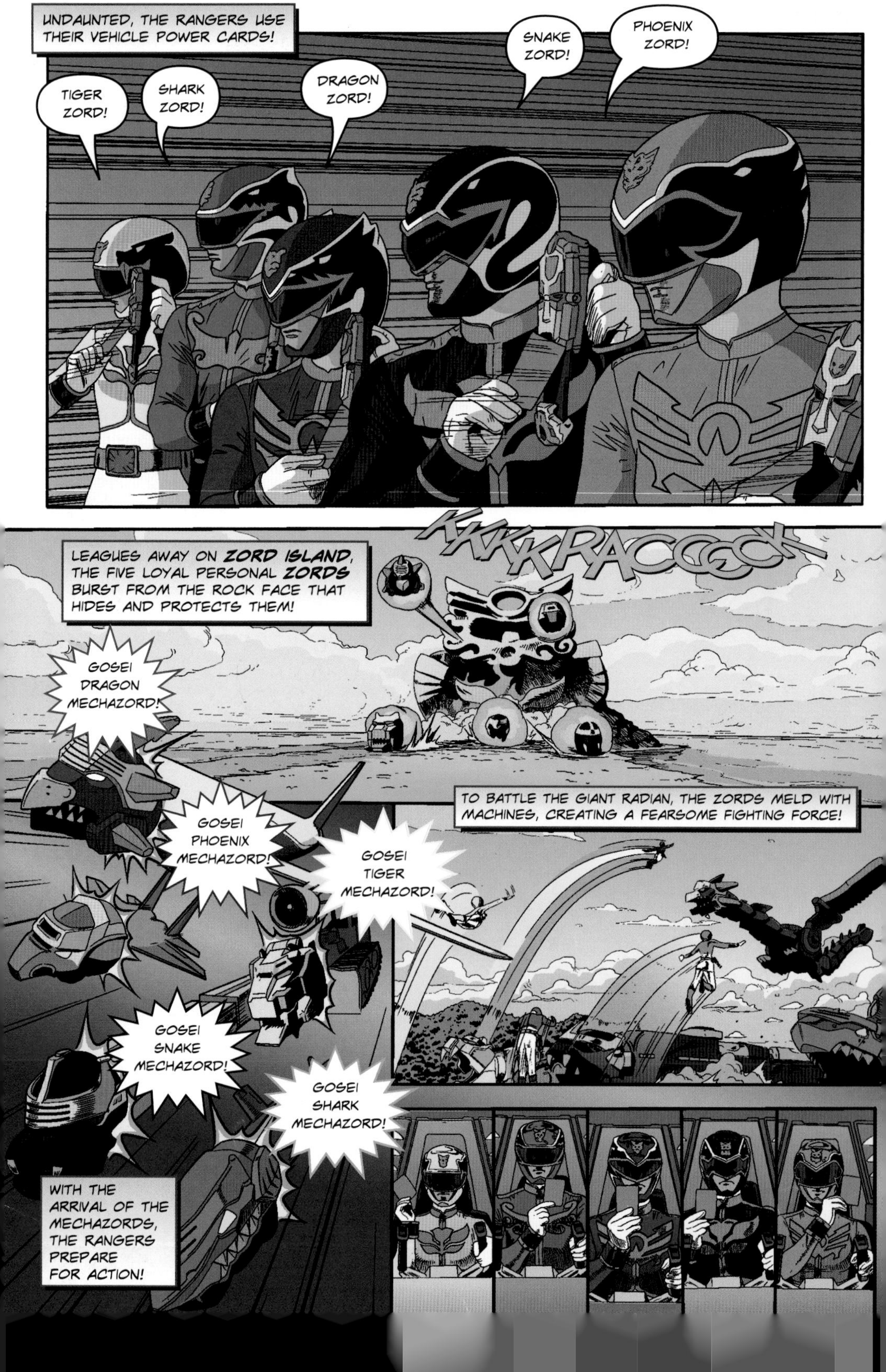
UNDAUNTED, THE RANGERS USE THEIR VEHICLE POWER CARDS!
TIGER ZORD!
SHARK ZORD!
DRAGON ZORD!
SNAKE ZORD!
PHOENIX ZORD!
KKKKRACCCCK
LEAGUES AWAY ON ZORD ISLAND, THE FIVE LOYAL PERSONAL ZORDS BURST FROM THE ROCK FACE THAT HIDES AND PROTECTS THEM!
GOSEI DRAGON MECHAZORD!
GOSEI PHOENIX MECHAZORD!
GOSEI TIGER MECHAZORD!
GOSEI SNAKE MECHAZORD!
GOSEI SHARK MECHAZORD!
TO BATTLE THE GIANT RADIAN, THE ZORDS MELD WITH MACHINES, CREATING A FEARSOME FIGHTING FORCE!
WITH THE ARRIVAL OF THE MECHAZORDS, THE RANGERS PREPARE FOR ACTION!

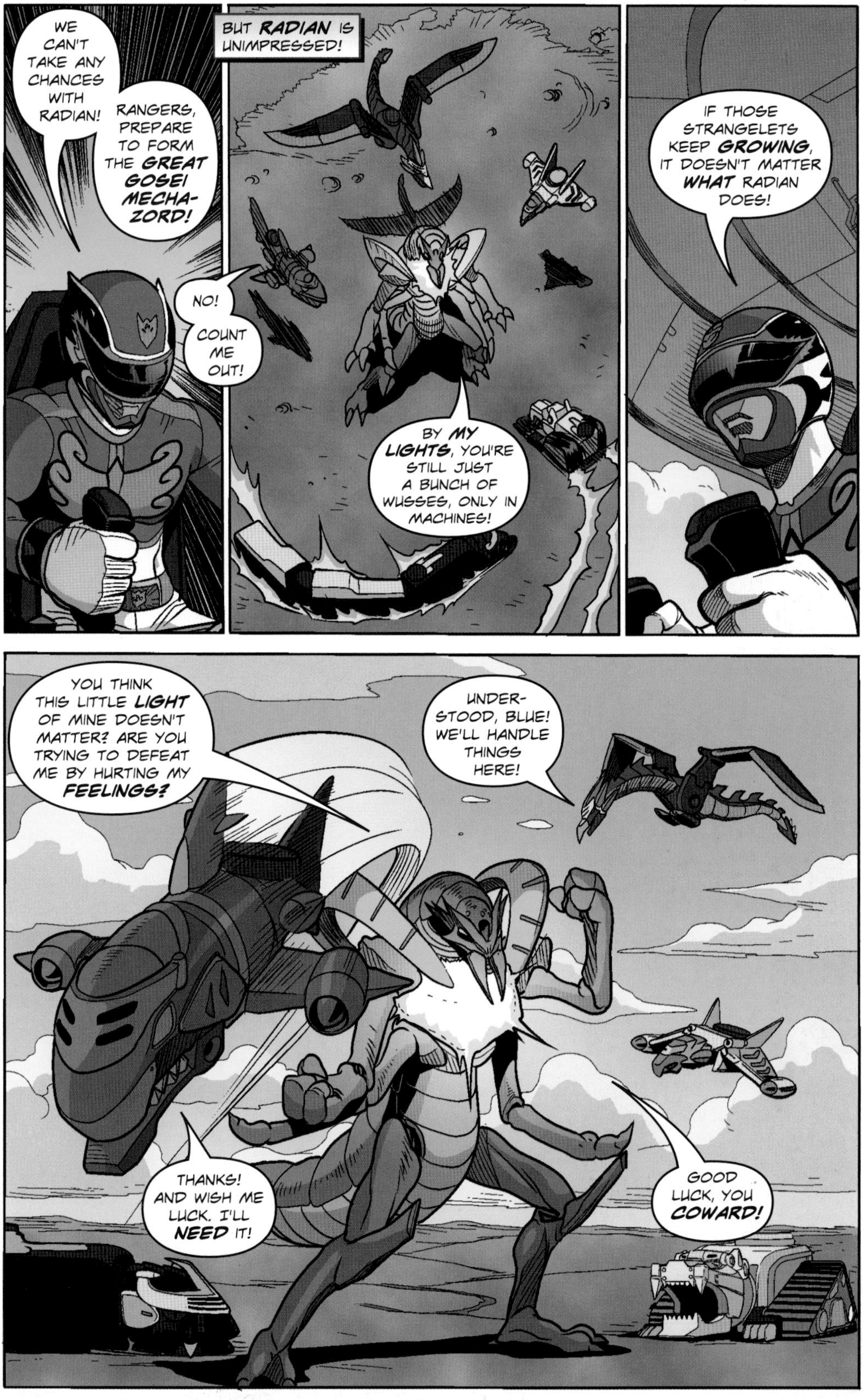
WE CAN'T TAKE ANY CHANCES WITH RADIAN!
RANGERS, PREPARE TO FORM THE GREAT GOSEI MECHAZORD!
NO!
COUNT ME OUT!
BUT RADIAN IS UNIMPRESSED!
BY MY LIGHTS, YOU'RE STILL JUST A BUNCH OF WUSSES, ONLY IN MACHINES!
IF THOSE STRANGELETS KEEP GROWING, IT DOESN'T MATTER WHAT RADIAN DOES!
YOU THINK THIS LITTLE LIGHT OF MINE DOESN'T MATTER? ARE YOU TRYING TO DEFEAT ME BY HURTING MY FEELINGS?
UNDERSTOOD, BLUE! WE'LL HANDLE THINGS HERE!
THANKS! AND WISH ME LUCK. I'LL NEED IT!
GOOD LUCK, YOU COWARD!

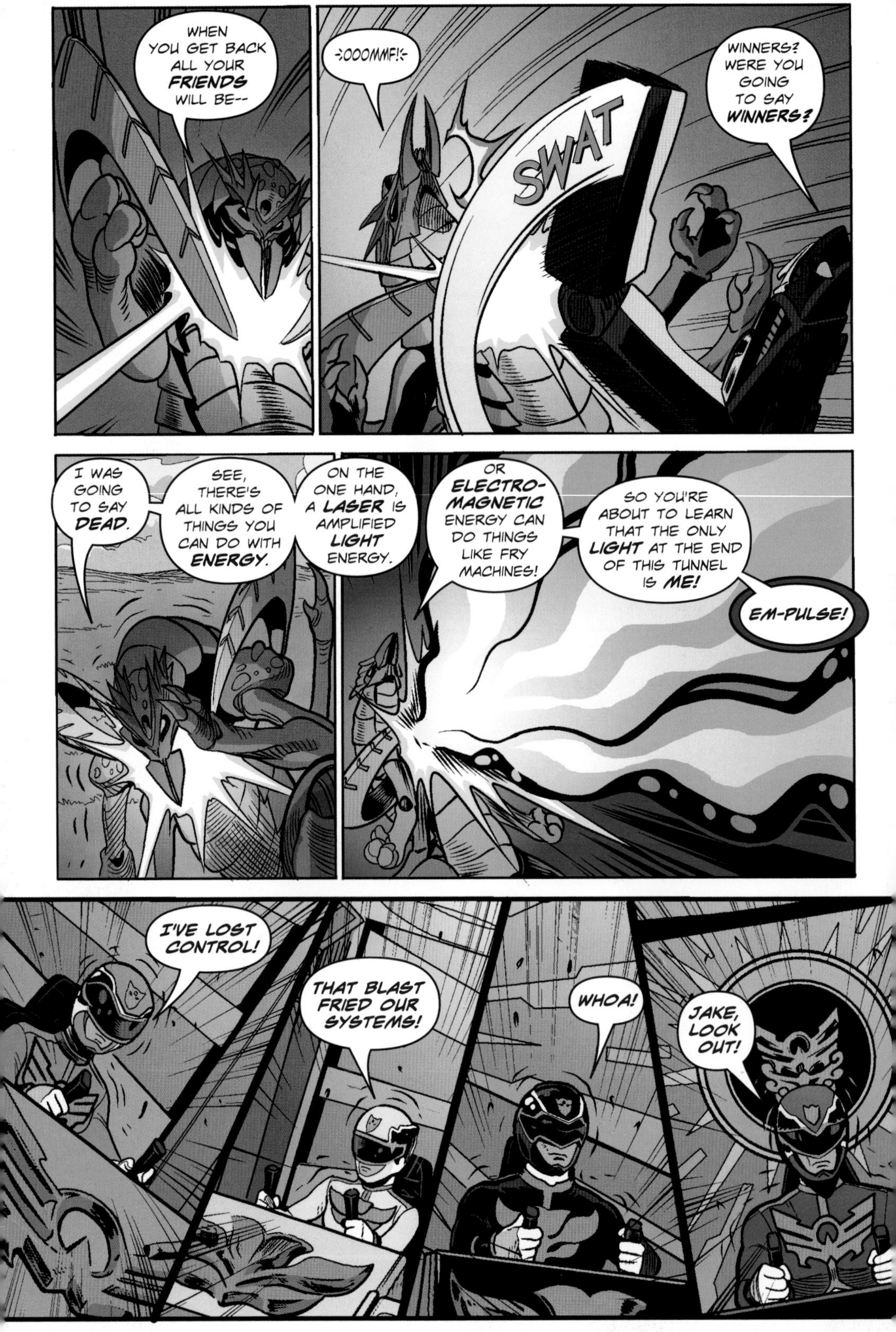
WHEN YOU GET BACK ALL YOUR FRIENDS WILL BE--
-:OOOMMF!:-
SWAT
WINNERS? WERE YOU GOING TO SAY WINNERS?
I WAS GOING TO SAY DEAD.
SEE, THERE'S ALL KINDS OF THINGS YOU CAN DO WITH ENERGY.
ON THE ONE HAND, A LASER IS AMPLIFIED LIGHT ENERGY.
OR ELECTRO-MAGNETIC ENERGY CAN DO THINGS LIKE FRY MACHINES!
SO YOU'RE ABOUT TO LEARN THAT THE ONLY LIGHT AT THE END OF THIS TUNNEL IS ME!
EM-PULSE!
I'VE LOST CONTROL!
THAT BLAST FRIED OUR SYSTEMS!
WHOA!
JAKE, LOOK OUT!

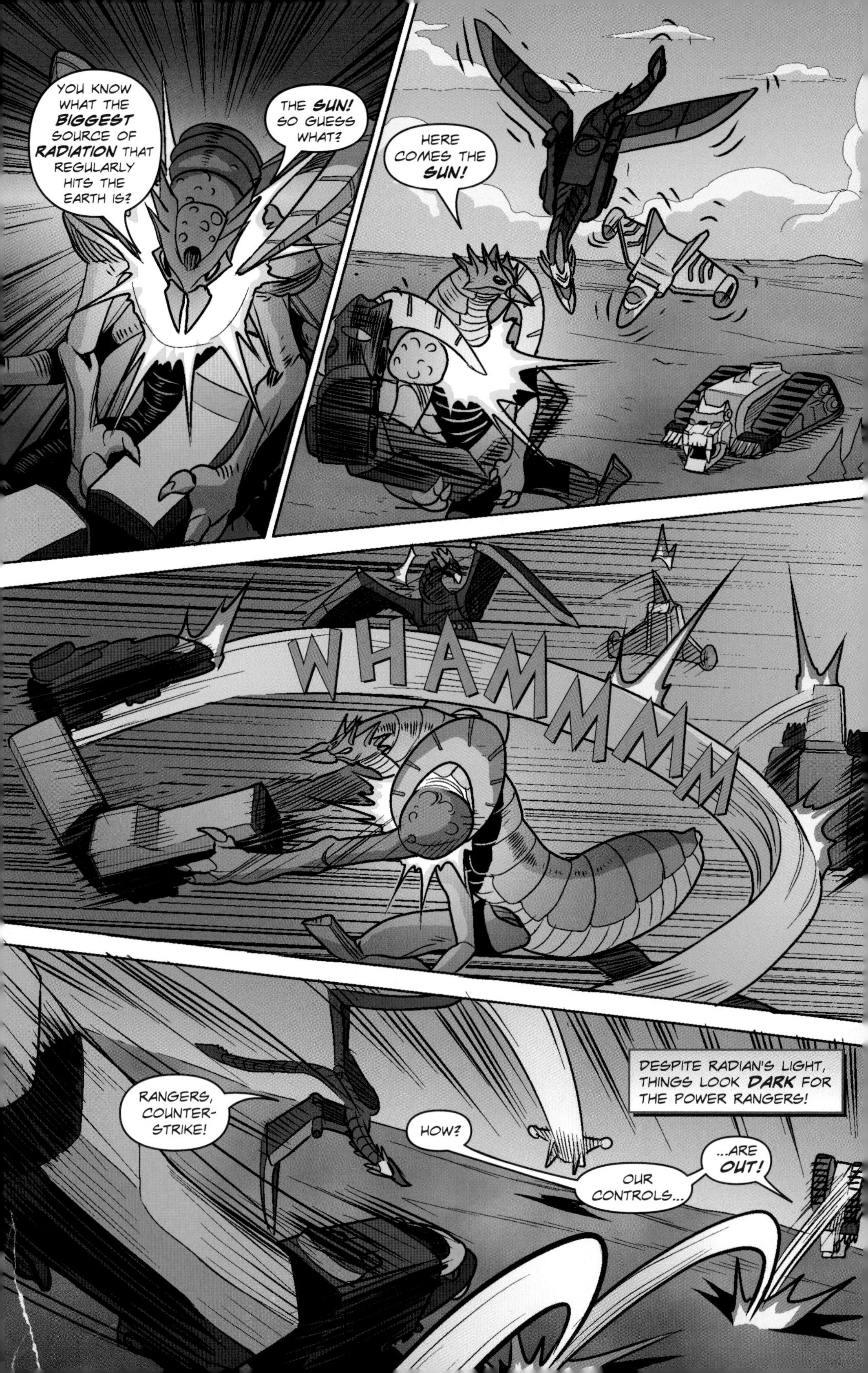
YOU KNOW WHAT THE BIGGEST SOURCE OF RADIATION THAT REGULARLY HITS THE EARTH IS?
THE SUN! SO GUESS WHAT?
HERE COMES THE SUN!
WHAMMMMM
DESPITE RADIAN'S LIGHT, THINGS LOOK DARK FOR THE POWER RANGERS!
RANGERS, COUNTER-STRIKE!
HOW?
OUR CONTROLS...
...ARE OUT!

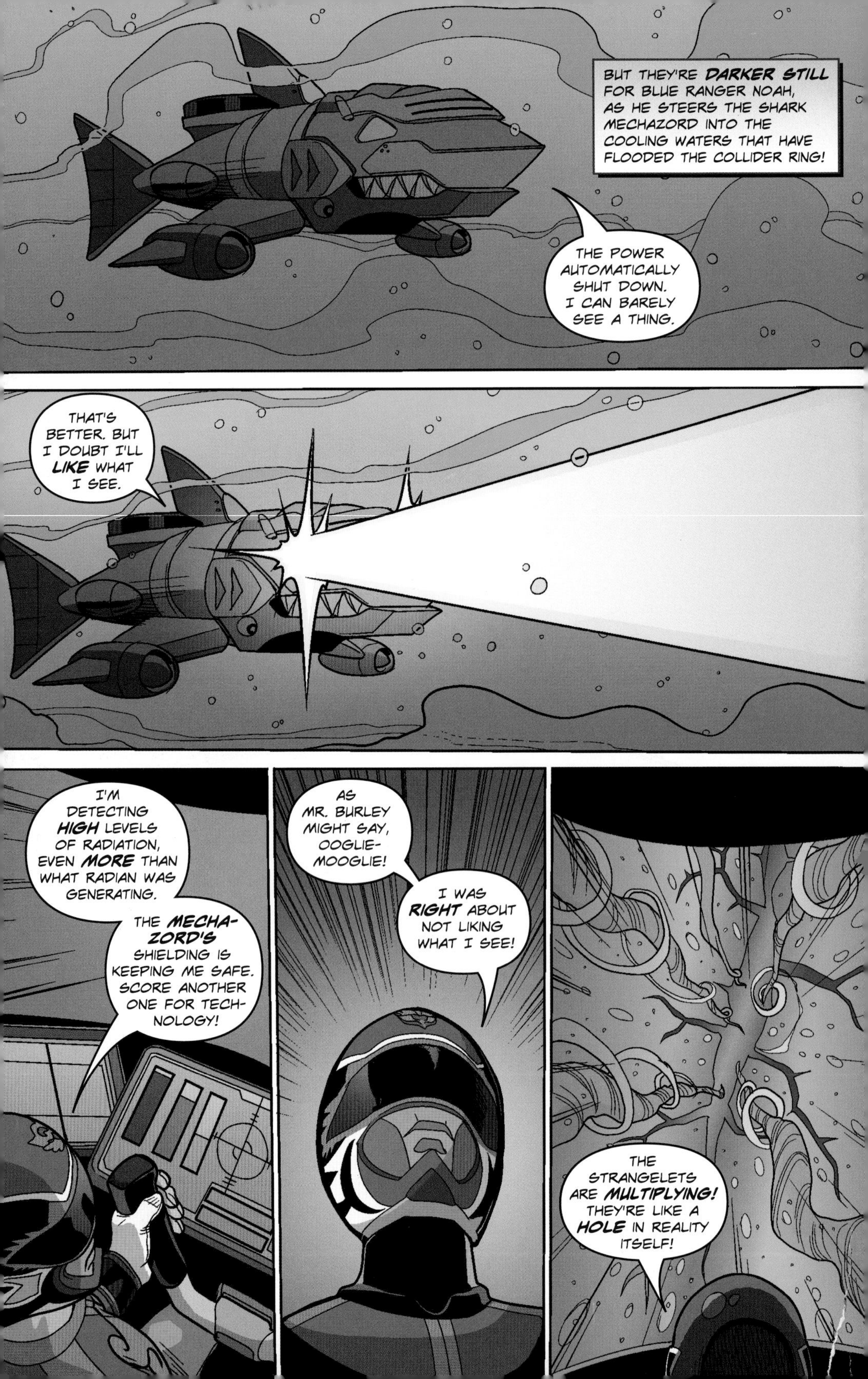

BUT THEY'RE DARKER STILL FOR BLUE RANGER NOAH, AS HE STEERS THE SHARK MECHAZORD INTO THE COOLING WATERS THAT HAVE FLOODED THE COLLIDER RING!
THE POWER AUTOMATICALLY SHUT DOWN. I CAN BARELY SEE A THING.
THAT'S BETTER. BUT I DOUBT I'LL LIKE WHAT I SEE.
I'M DETECTING HIGH LEVELS OF RADIATION, EVEN MORE THAN WHAT RADIAN WAS GENERATING.
THE MECHAZORD'S SHIELDING IS KEEPING ME SAFE. SCORE ANOTHER ONE FOR TECHNOLOGY!
AS MR. BURLEY MIGHT SAY, OOGLIE-MOOGLIE!
I WAS RIGHT ABOUT NOT LIKING WHAT I SEE!
THE STRANGELETS ARE MULTIPLYING! THEY'RE LIKE A HOLE IN REALITY ITSELF!

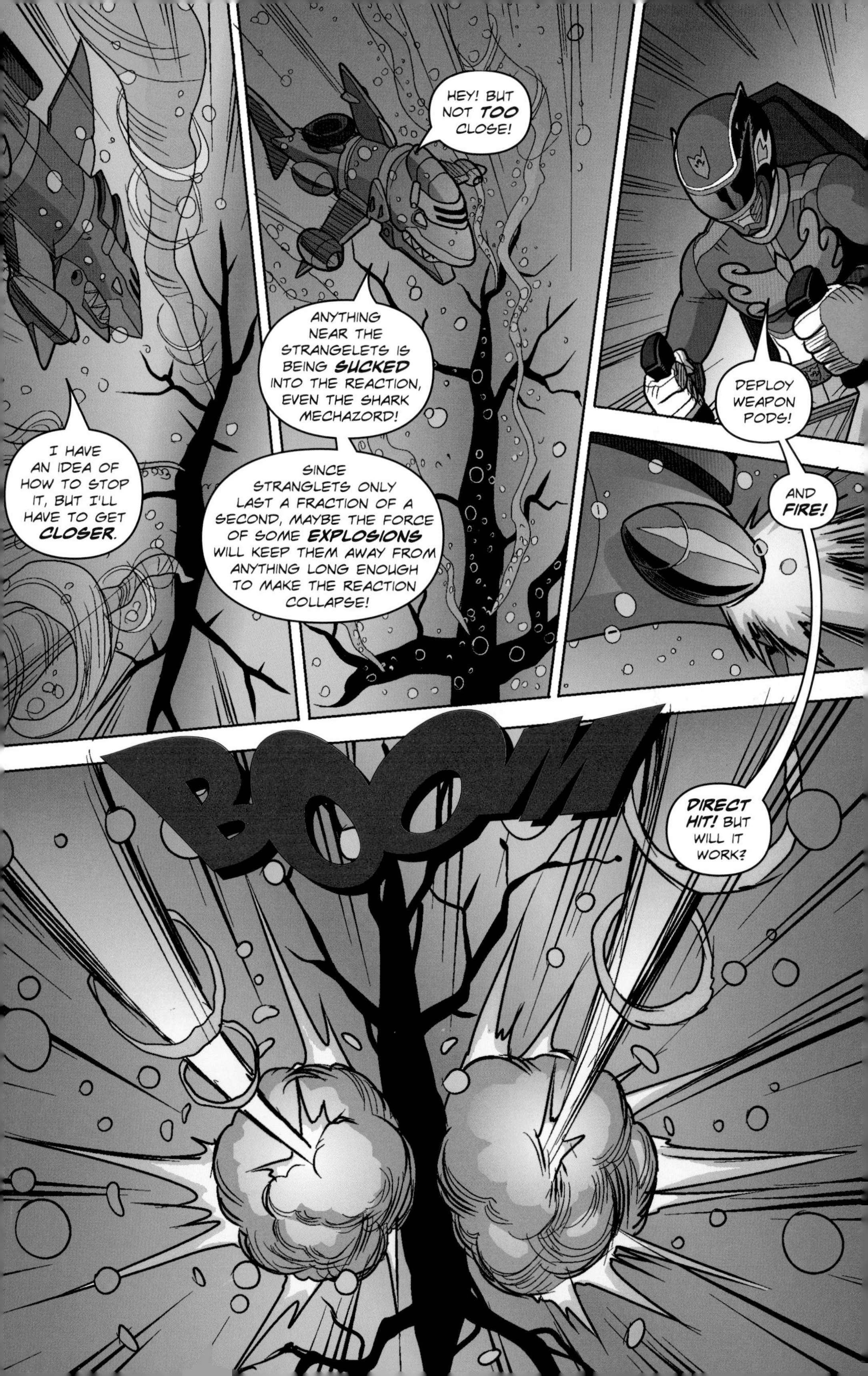
I HAVE AN IDEA OF HOW TO STOP IT, BUT I'LL HAVE TO GET **CLOSER**.
HEY! BUT NOT **TOO** CLOSE!
ANYTHING NEAR THE STRANGELETS IS BEING **SUCKED** INTO THE REACTION, EVEN THE SHARK MECHAZORD!
SINCE STRANGLETS ONLY LAST A FRACTION OF A SECOND, MAYBE THE FORCE OF SOME **EXPLOSIONS** WILL KEEP THEM AWAY FROM ANYTHING LONG ENOUGH TO MAKE THE REACTION COLLAPSE!
DEPLOY WEAPON PODS!
AND **FIRE!**
BOOM
DIRECT HIT! BUT WILL IT WORK?

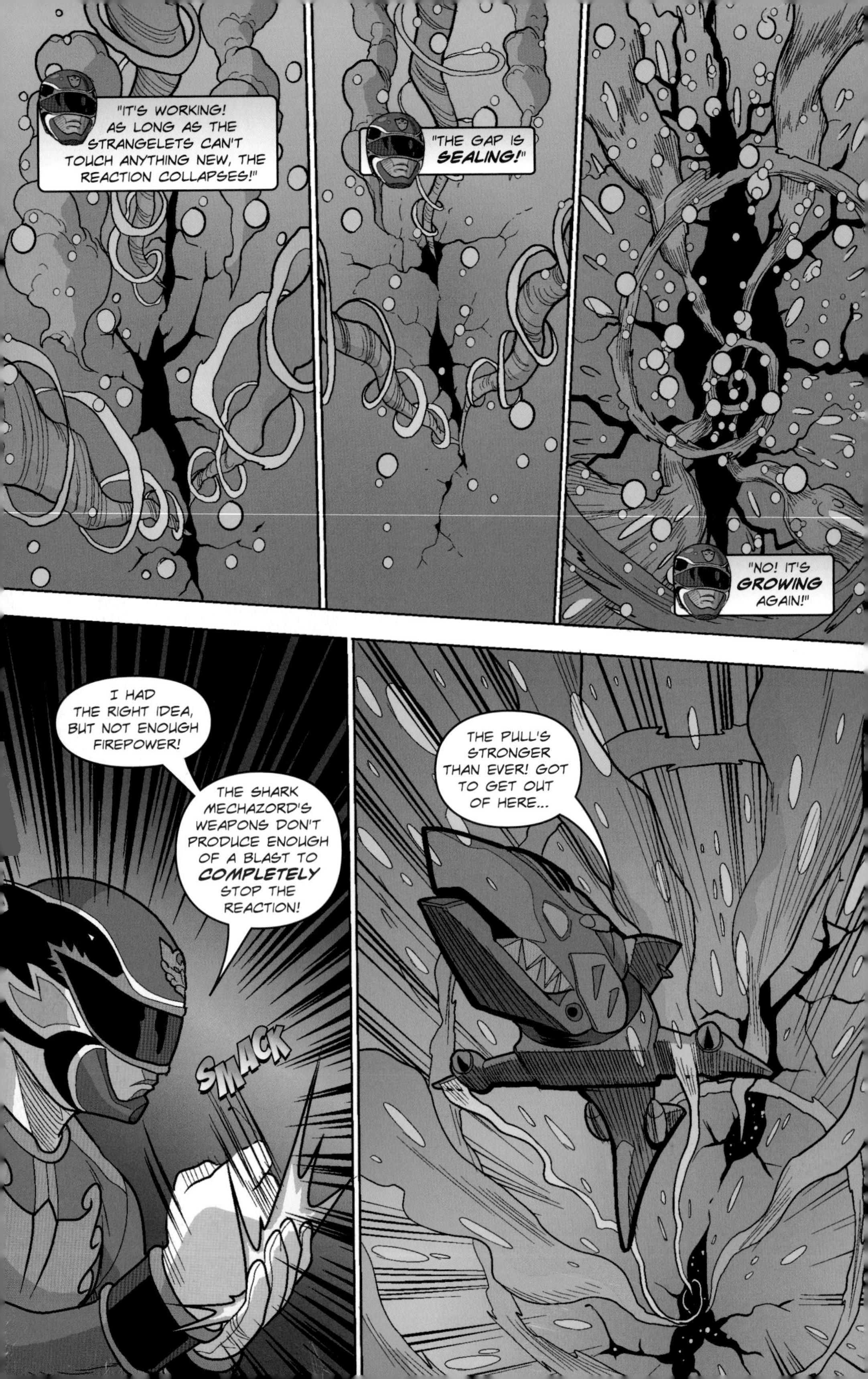
"IT'S WORKING! AS LONG AS THE STRANGELETS CAN'T TOUCH ANYTHING NEW, THE REACTION COLLAPSES!"
"THE GAP IS SEALING!"
"NO! IT'S GROWING AGAIN!"
I HAD THE RIGHT IDEA, BUT NOT ENOUGH FIREPOWER!
THE SHARK MECHAZORD'S WEAPONS DON'T PRODUCE ENOUGH OF A BLAST TO COMPLETELY STOP THE REACTION!
SMACK
THE PULL'S STRONGER THAN EVER! GOT TO GET OUT OF HERE...

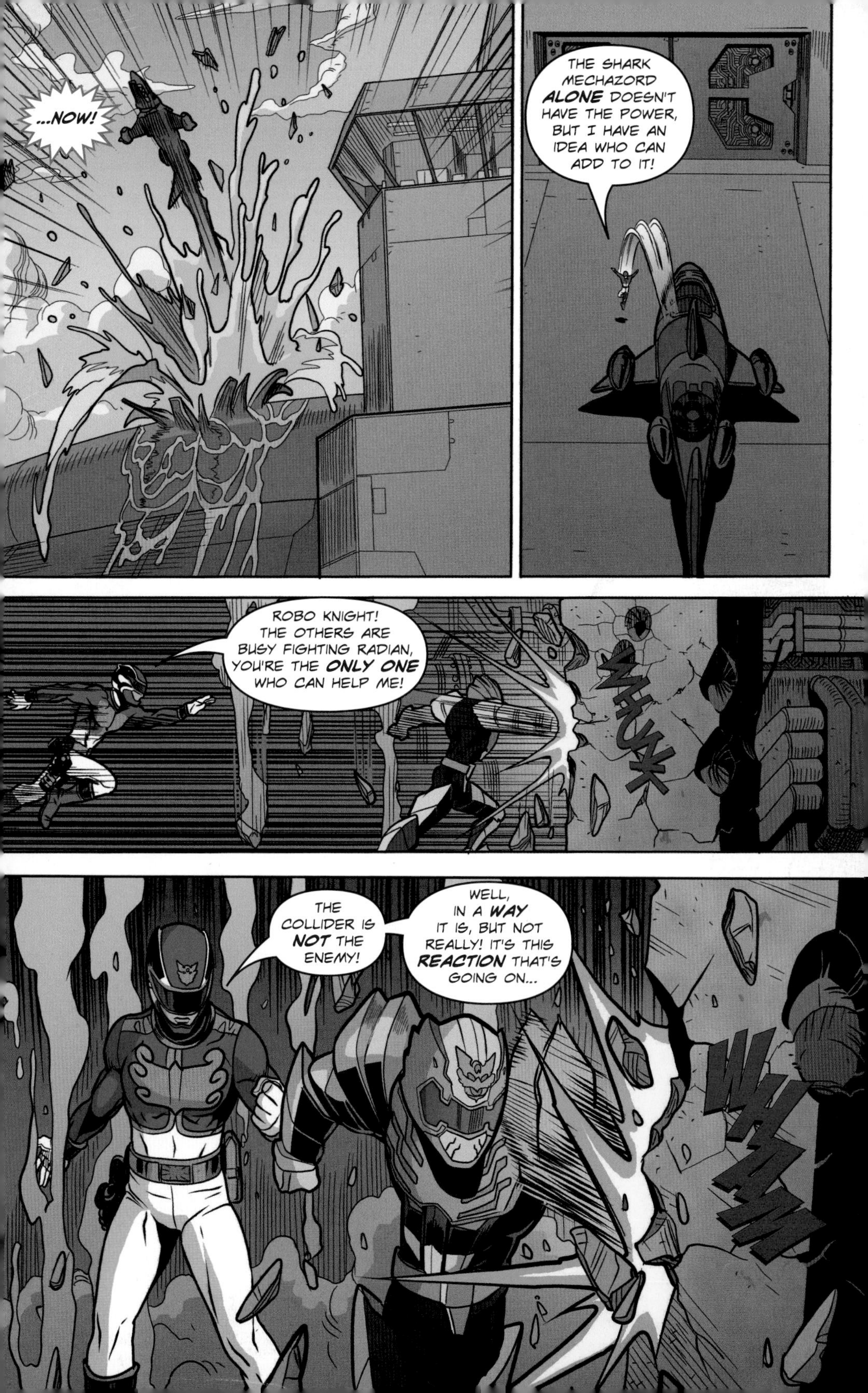
...NOW!
THE SHARK MECHAZORD ALONE DOESN'T HAVE THE POWER, BUT I HAVE AN IDEA WHO CAN ADD TO IT!
ROBO KNIGHT! THE OTHERS ARE BUSY FIGHTING RADIAN, YOU'RE THE ONLY ONE WHO CAN HELP ME!
WHUNK
THE COLLIDER IS NOT THE ENEMY!
WELL, IN A WAY IT IS, BUT NOT REALLY! IT'S THIS REACTION THAT'S GOING ON...
WHAMM

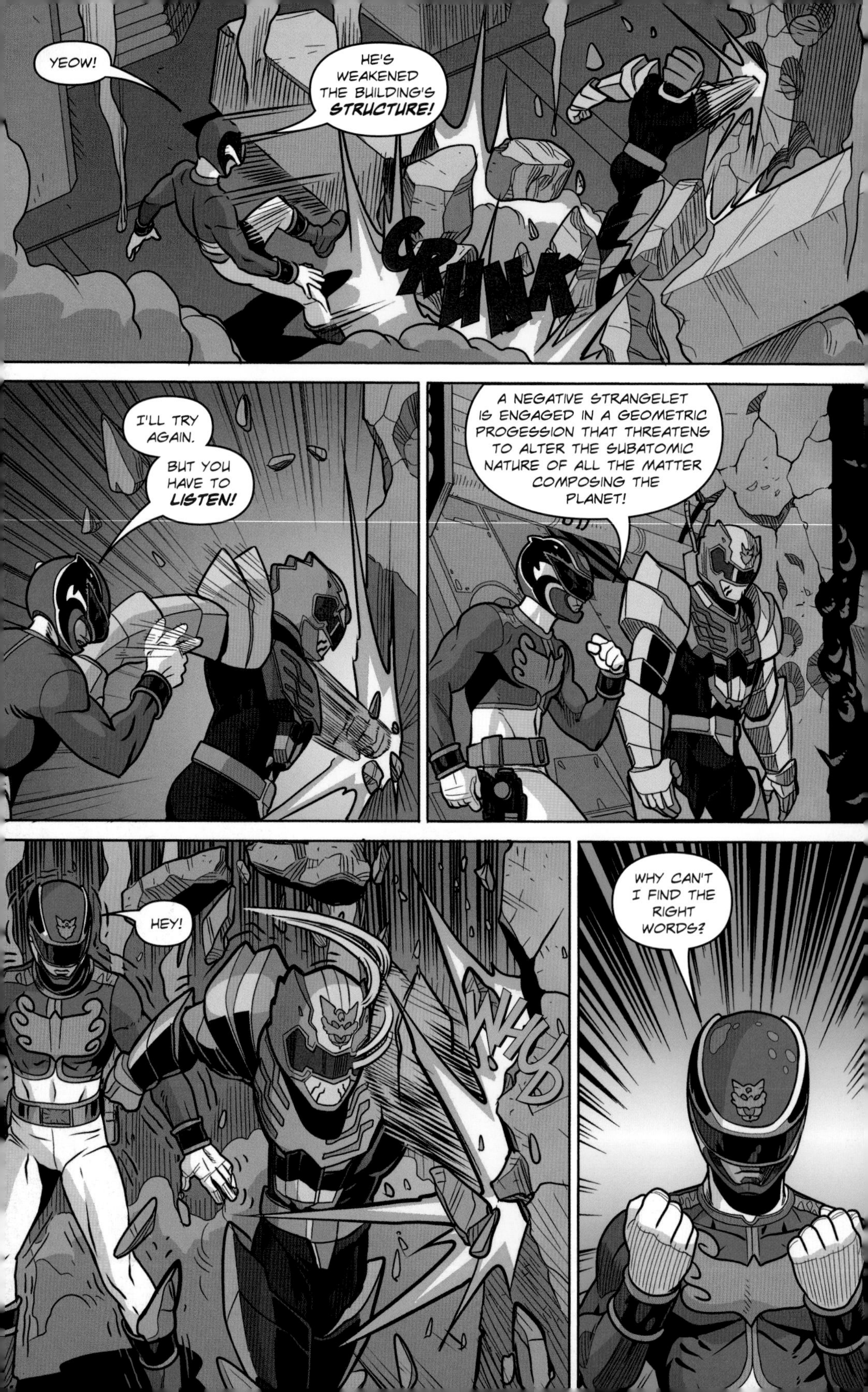
YEOW!
HE'S WEAKENED THE BUILDING'S STRUCTURE!
CRUNK
I'LL TRY AGAIN.
BUT YOU HAVE TO LISTEN!
A NEGATIVE STRANGELET IS ENGAGED IN A GEOMETRIC PROGESSION THAT THREATENS TO ALTER THE SUBATOMIC NATURE OF ALL THE MATTER COMPOSING THE PLANET!
HEY!
WHUD
WHY CAN'T I FIND THE RIGHT WORDS?

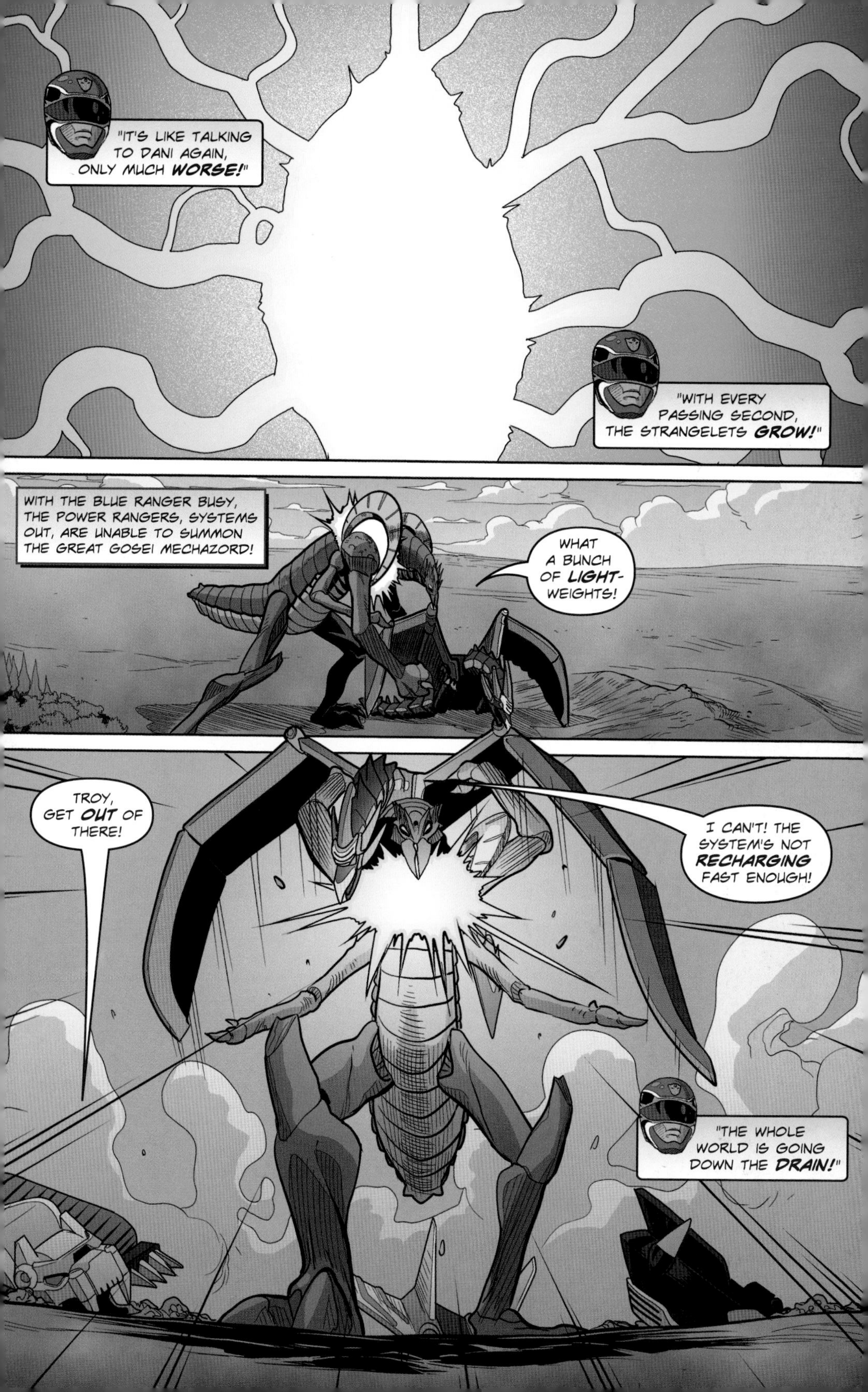
"IT'S LIKE TALKING TO DANI AGAIN, ONLY MUCH WORSE!"
"WITH EVERY PASSING SECOND, THE STRANGELETS GROW!"
WITH THE BLUE RANGER BUSY, THE POWER RANGERS, SYSTEMS OUT, ARE UNABLE TO SUMMON THE GREAT GOSEI MECHAZORD!
WHAT A BUNCH OF LIGHT-WEIGHTS!
TROY, GET OUT OF THERE!
I CAN'T! THE SYSTEM'S NOT RECHARGING FAST ENOUGH!
"THE WHOLE WORLD IS GOING DOWN THE DRAIN!"

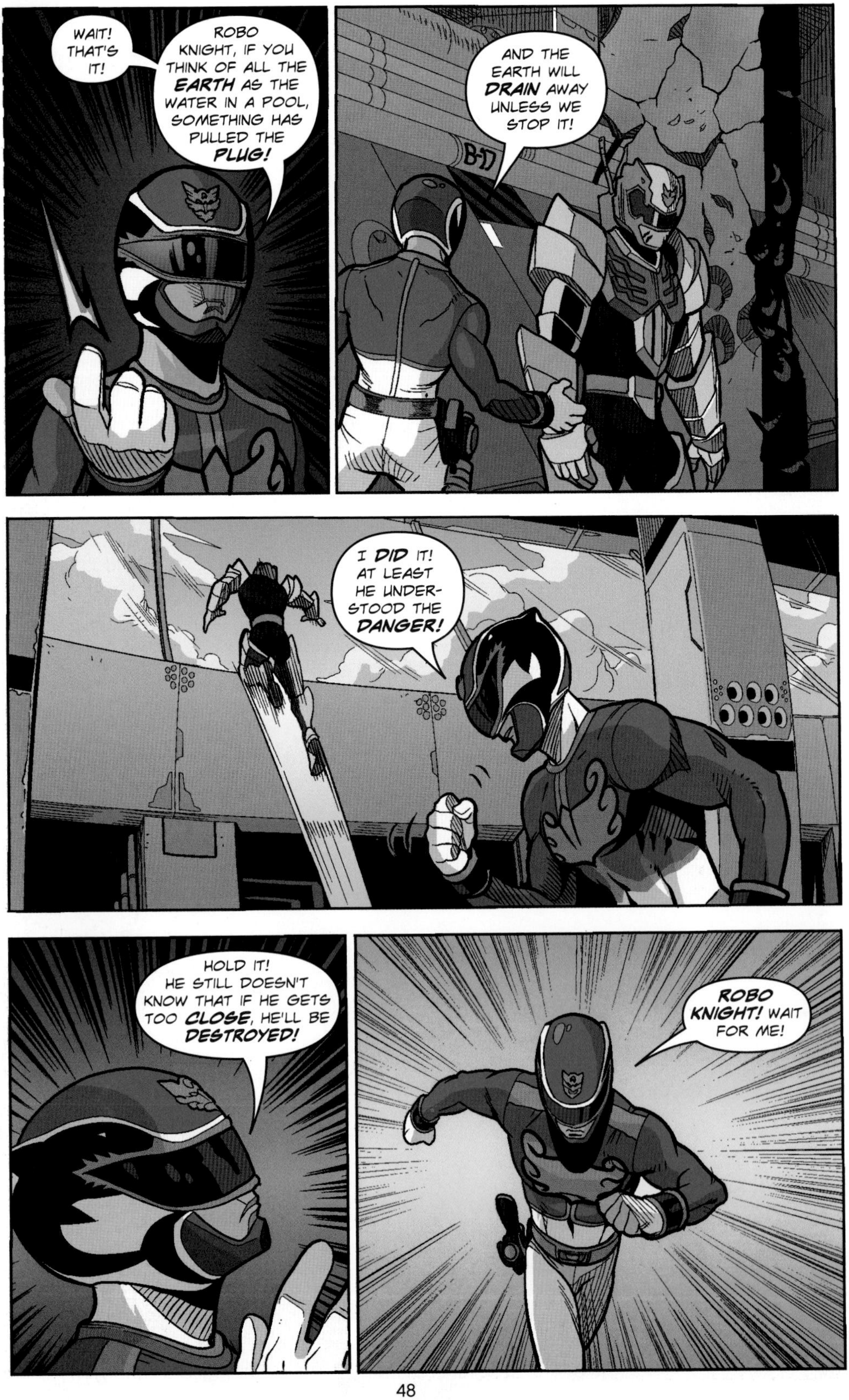
WAIT! THAT'S IT!
ROBO KNIGHT, IF YOU THINK OF ALL THE EARTH AS THE WATER IN A POOL, SOMETHING HAS PULLED THE PLUG!
AND THE EARTH WILL DRAIN AWAY UNLESS WE STOP IT!
B-D
I DID IT! AT LEAST HE UNDERSTOOD THE DANGER!
HOLD IT! HE STILL DOESN'T KNOW THAT IF HE GETS TOO CLOSE, HE'LL BE DESTROYED!
ROBO KNIGHT! WAIT FOR ME!

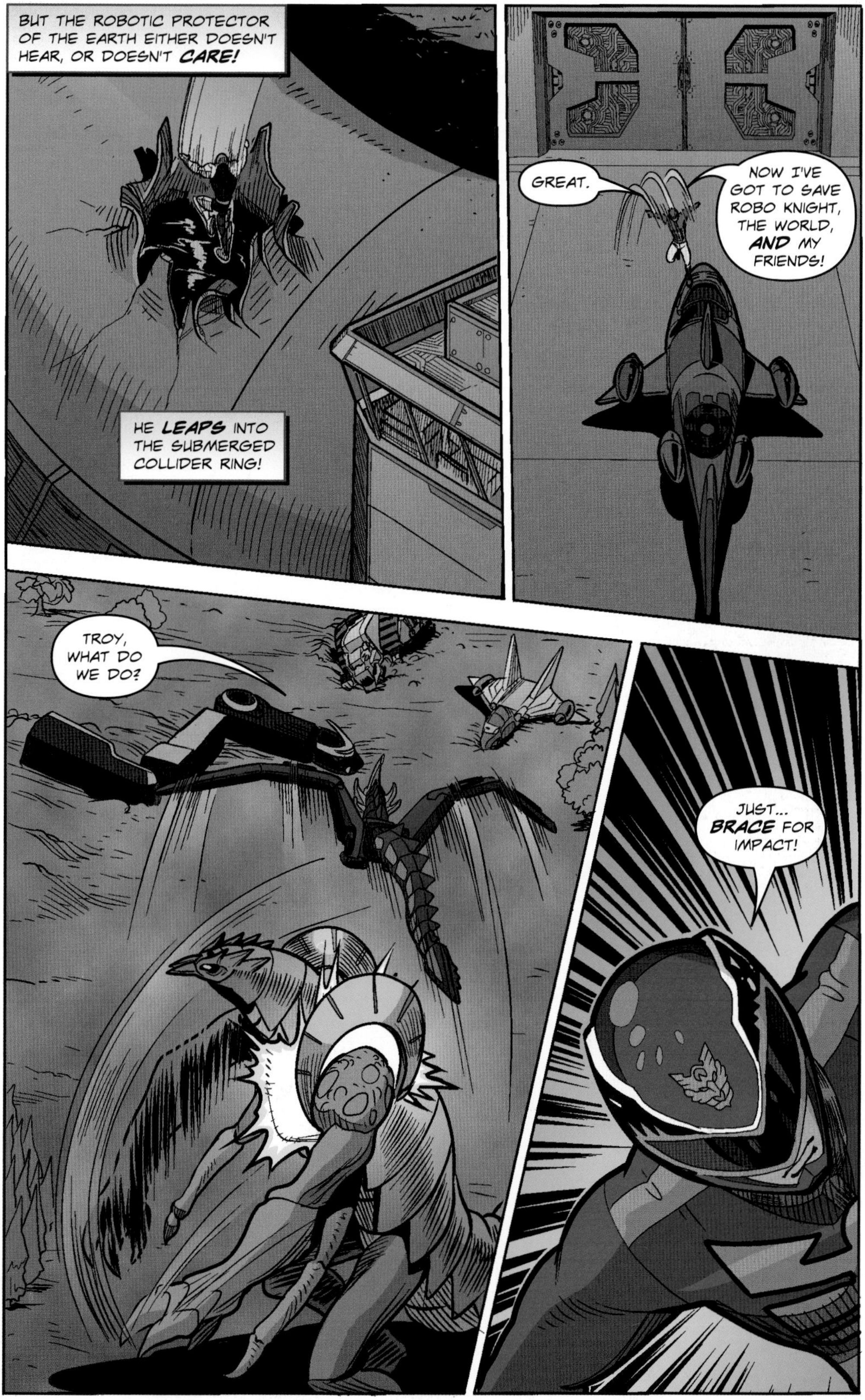
BUT THE ROBOTIC PROTECTOR OF THE EARTH EITHER DOESN'T HEAR, OR DOESN'T CARE!
HE LEAPS INTO THE SUBMERGED COLLIDER RING!
GREAT.
NOW I'VE GOT TO SAVE ROBO KNIGHT, THE WORLD, AND MY FRIENDS!
TROY, WHAT DO WE DO?
JUST... BRACE FOR IMPACT!

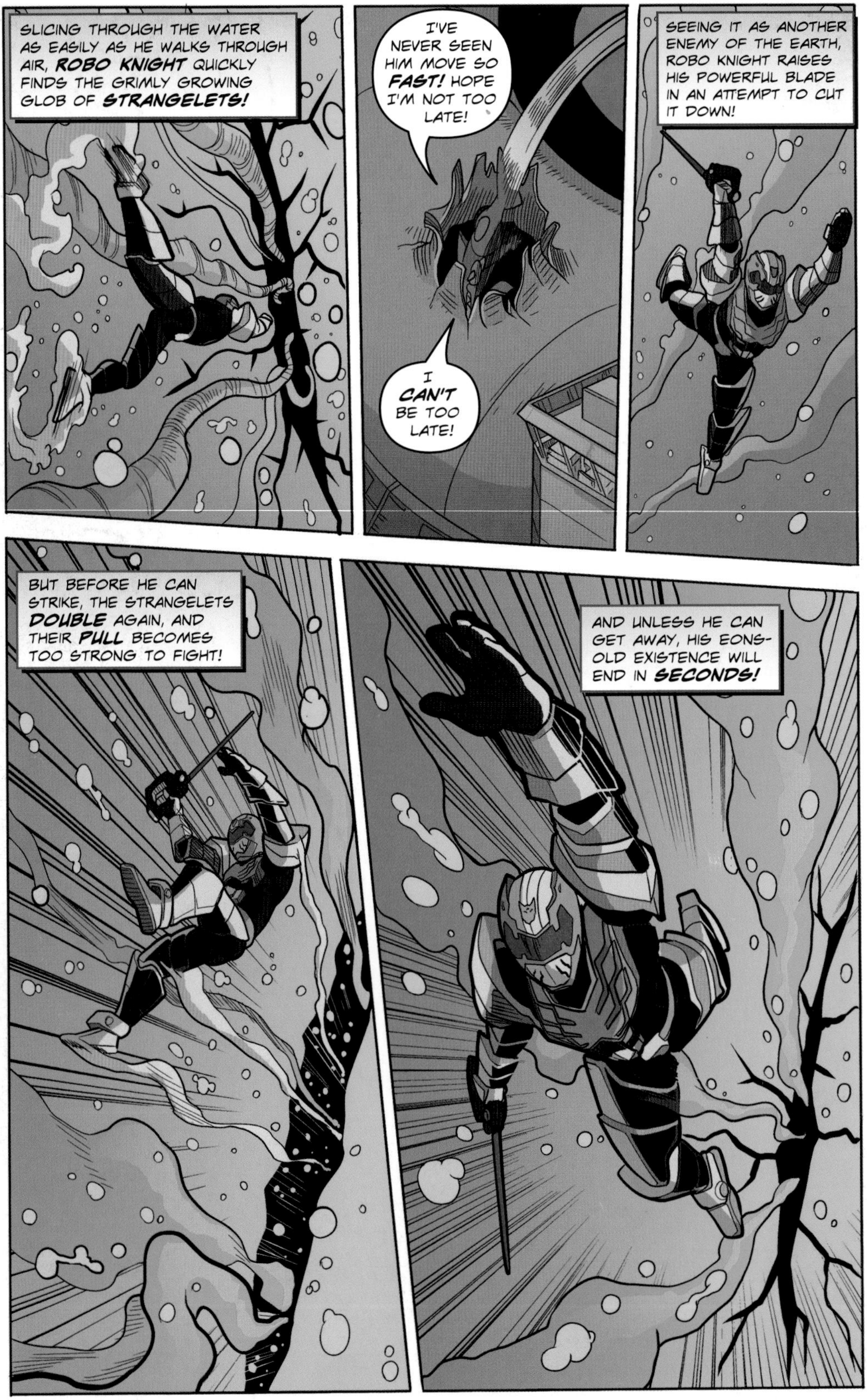
SLICING THROUGH THE WATER AS EASILY AS HE WALKS THROUGH AIR, ROBO KNIGHT QUICKLY FINDS THE GRIMLY GROWING GLOB OF STRANGELETS!
I'VE NEVER SEEN HIM MOVE SO FAST! HOPE I'M NOT TOO LATE!
I CAN'T BE TOO LATE!
SEEING IT AS ANOTHER ENEMY OF THE EARTH, ROBO KNIGHT RAISES HIS POWERFUL BLADE IN AN ATTEMPT TO CUT IT DOWN!
BUT BEFORE HE CAN STRIKE, THE STRANGELETS DOUBLE AGAIN, AND THEIR PULL BECOMES TOO STRONG TO FIGHT!
AND UNLESS HE CAN GET AWAY, HIS EONS-OLD EXISTENCE WILL END IN SECONDS!

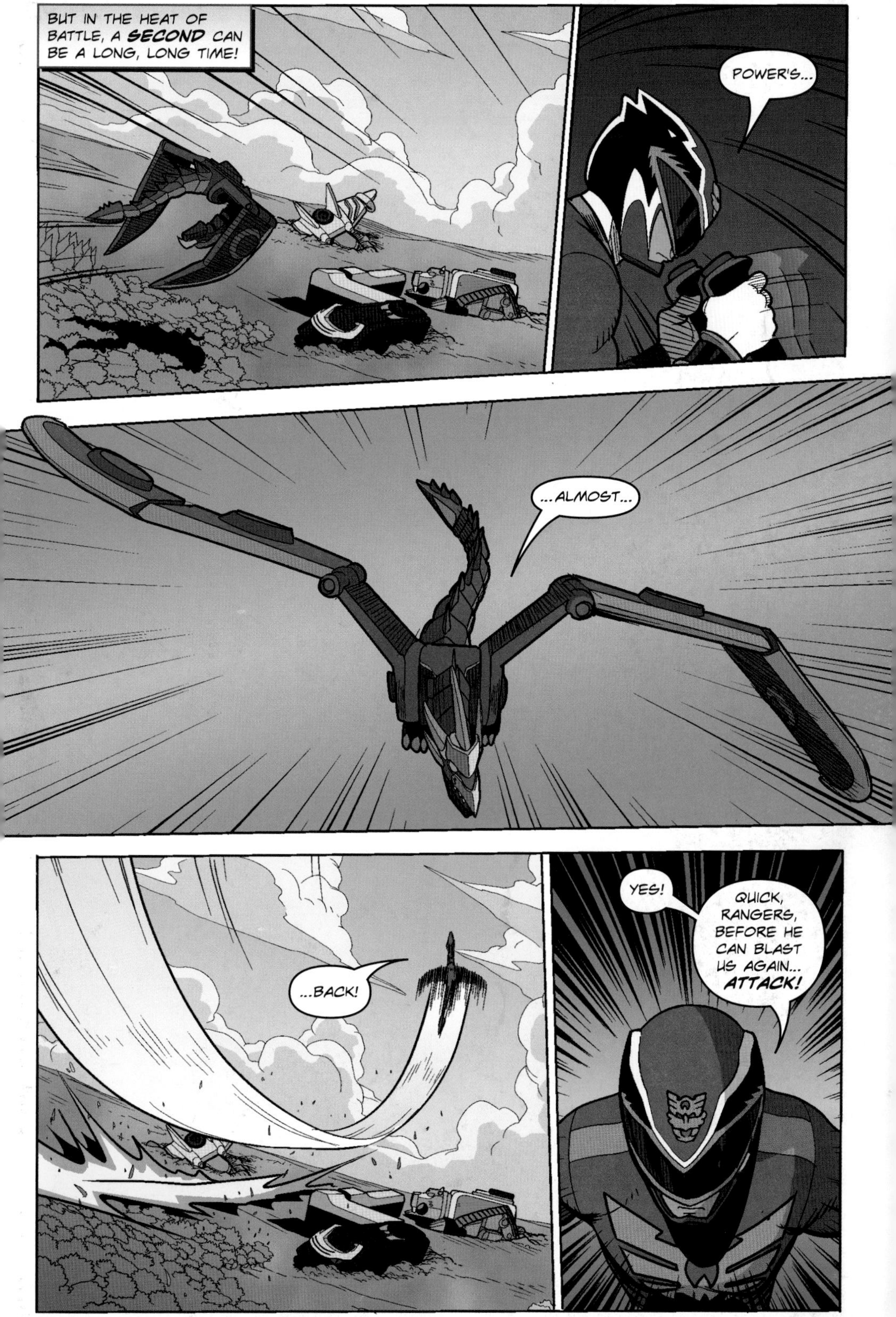
BUT IN THE HEAT OF BATTLE, A SECOND CAN BE A LONG, LONG TIME!
POWER'S...
...ALMOST...
...BACK!
YES!
QUICK, RANGERS, BEFORE HE CAN BLAST US AGAIN... ATTACK!

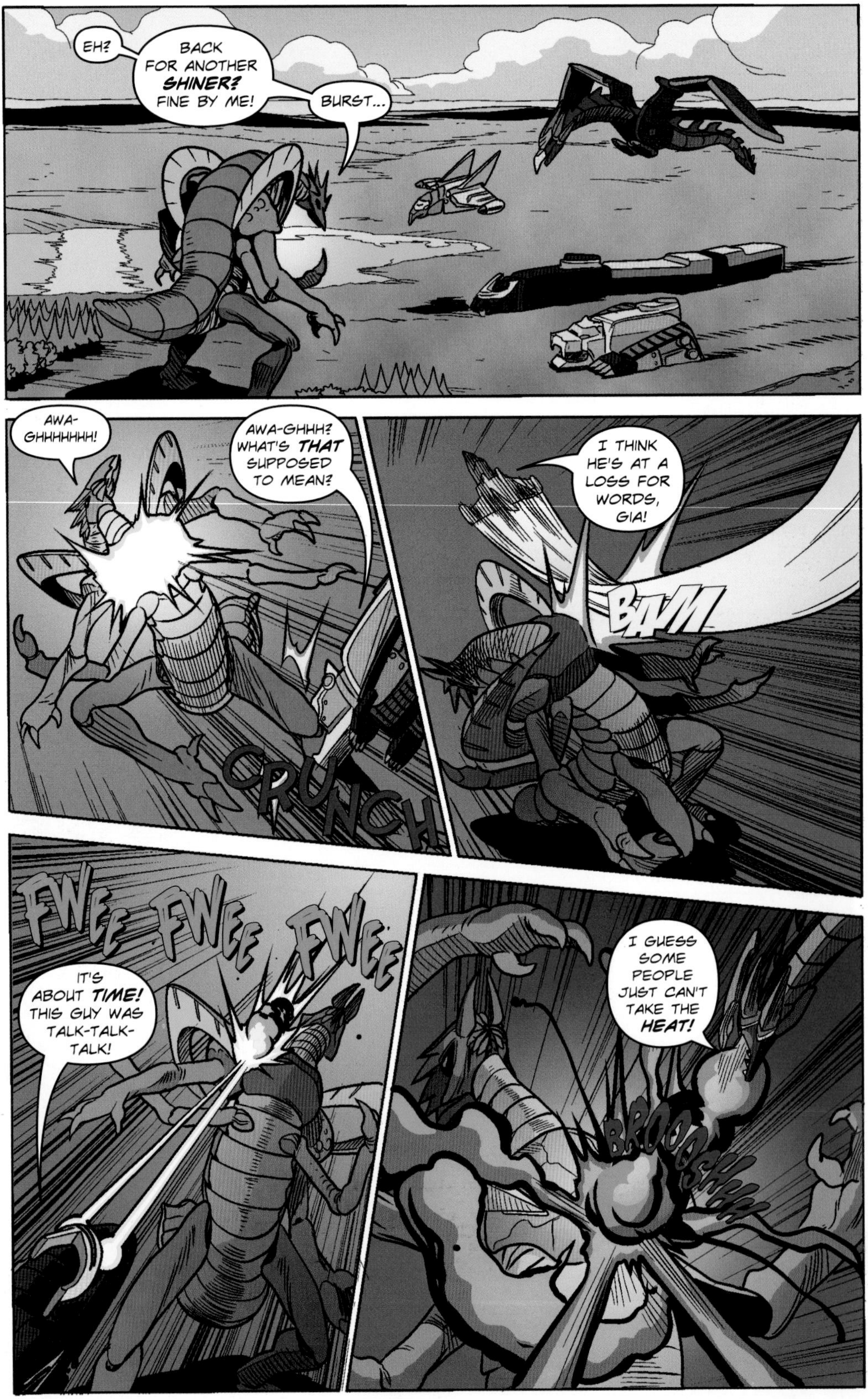
EH?
BACK FOR ANOTHER SHINER? FINE BY ME!
BURST...
AWA-GHHHHHHH!
AWA-GHHH? WHAT'S THAT SUPPOSED TO MEAN?
CRUNCH
I THINK HE'S AT A LOSS FOR WORDS, GIA!
BAM
FWEE FWEE FWEE
IT'S ABOUT TIME! THIS GUY WAS TALK-TALK-TALK!
I GUESS SOME PEOPLE JUST CAN'T TAKE THE HEAT!
BROOOSHHH

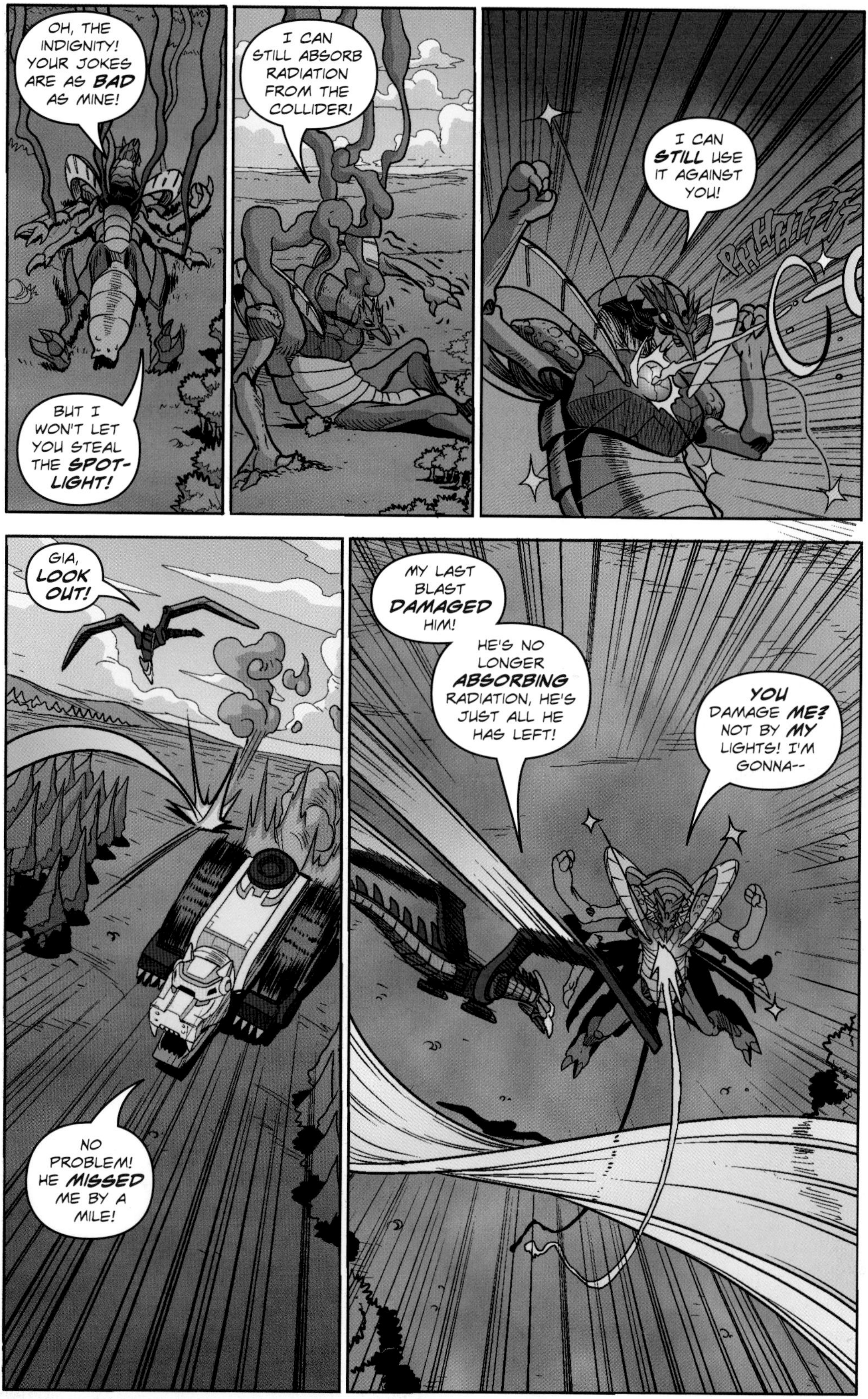
OH, THE INDIGNITY! YOUR JOKES ARE AS BAD AS MINE!
BUT I WON'T LET YOU STEAL THE SPOT-LIGHT!
I CAN STILL ABSORB RADIATION FROM THE COLLIDER!
I CAN STILL USE IT AGAINST YOU!
GIA, LOOK OUT!
NO PROBLEM! HE MISSED ME BY A MILE!
MY LAST BLAST DAMAGED HIM!
HE'S NO LONGER ABSORBING RADIATION, HE'S JUST ALL HE HAS LEFT!
YOU DAMAGE ME? NOT BY MY LIGHTS! I'M GONNA--

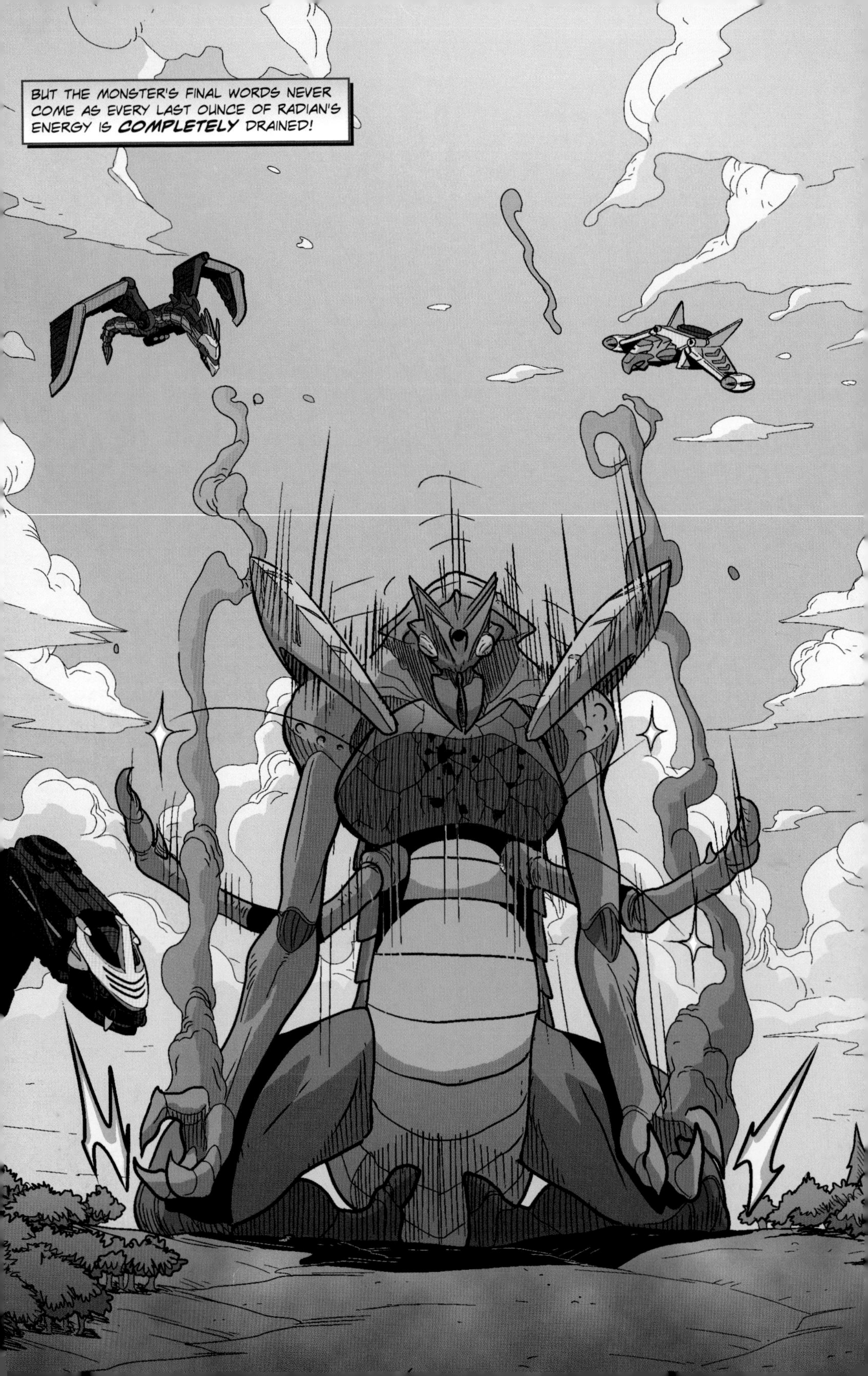
BUT THE MONSTER'S FINAL WORDS NEVER COME AS EVERY LAST OUNCE OF RADIAN'S ENERGY IS COMPLETELY DRAINED!

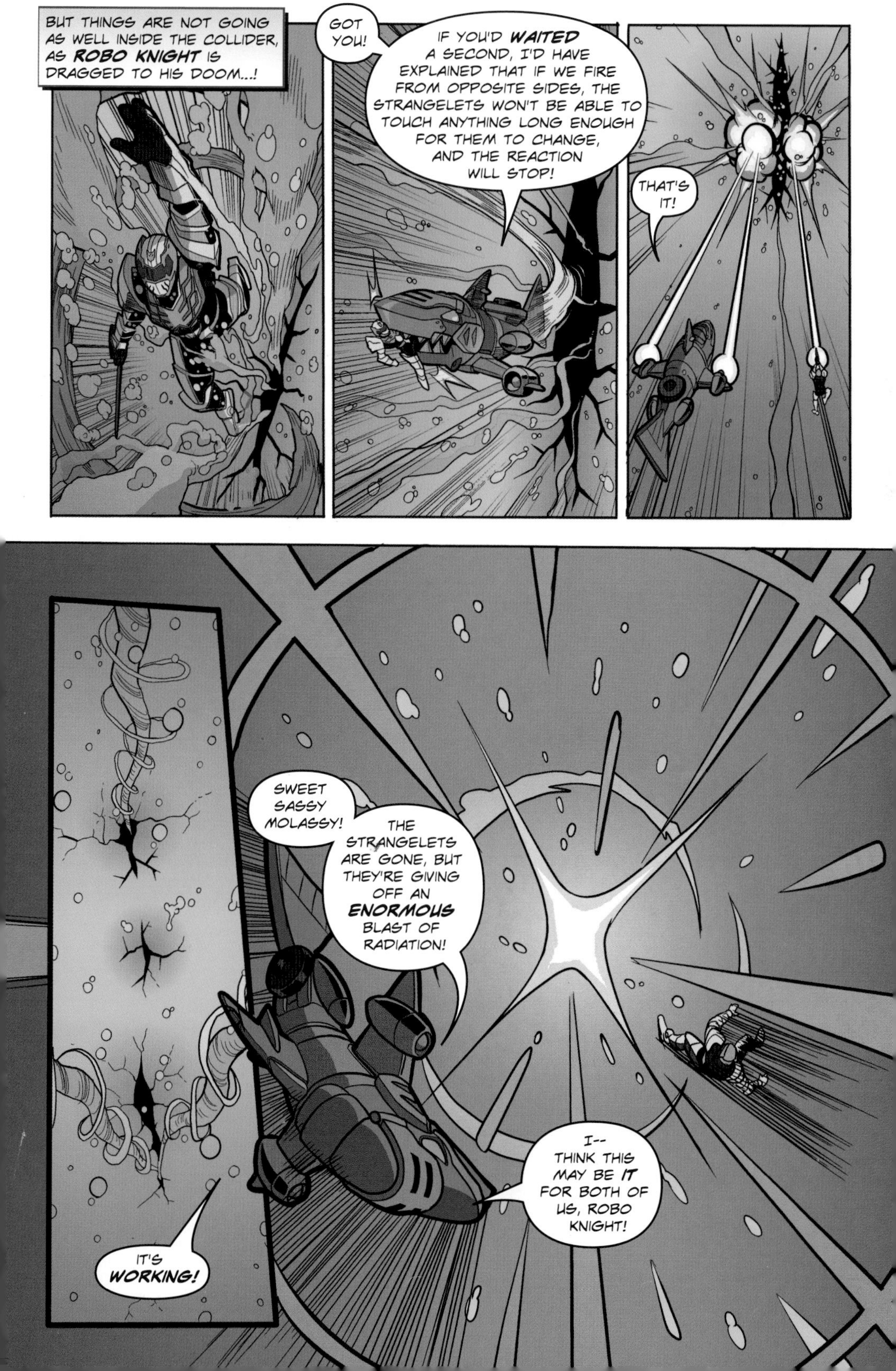
BUT THINGS ARE NOT GOING AS WELL INSIDE THE COLLIDER, AS ROBO KNIGHT IS DRAGGED TO HIS DOOM...!
GOT YOU!
IF YOU'D WAITED A SECOND, I'D HAVE EXPLAINED THAT IF WE FIRE FROM OPPOSITE SIDES, THE STRANGELETS WON'T BE ABLE TO TOUCH ANYTHING LONG ENOUGH FOR THEM TO CHANGE, AND THE REACTION WILL STOP!
THAT'S IT!
IT'S WORKING!
SWEET SASSY MOLASSY!
THE STRANGELETS ARE GONE, BUT THEY'RE GIVING OFF AN ENORMOUS BLAST OF RADIATION!
I-- THINK THIS MAY BE IT FOR BOTH OF US, ROBO KNIGHT!

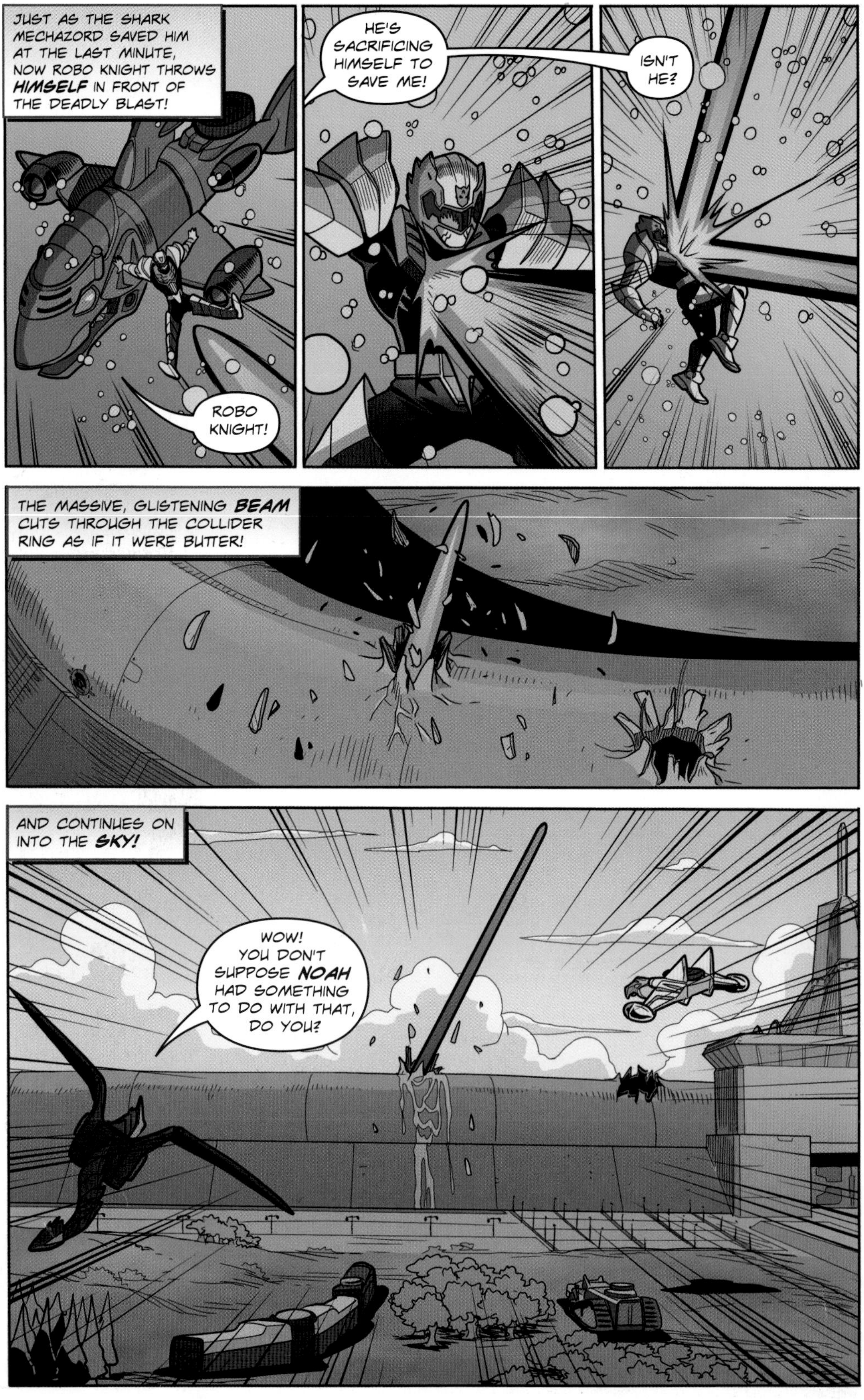
JUST AS THE SHARK MECHAZORD SAVED HIM AT THE LAST MINUTE, NOW ROBO KNIGHT THROWS HIMSELF IN FRONT OF THE DEADLY BLAST!
ROBO KNIGHT!
HE'S SACRIFICING HIMSELF TO SAVE ME!
ISN'T HE?
THE MASSIVE, GLISTENING BEAM CUTS THROUGH THE COLLIDER RING AS IF IT WERE BUTTER!
AND CONTINUES ON INTO THE SKY!
WOW! YOU DON'T SUPPOSE NOAH HAD SOMETHING TO DO WITH THAT, DO YOU?

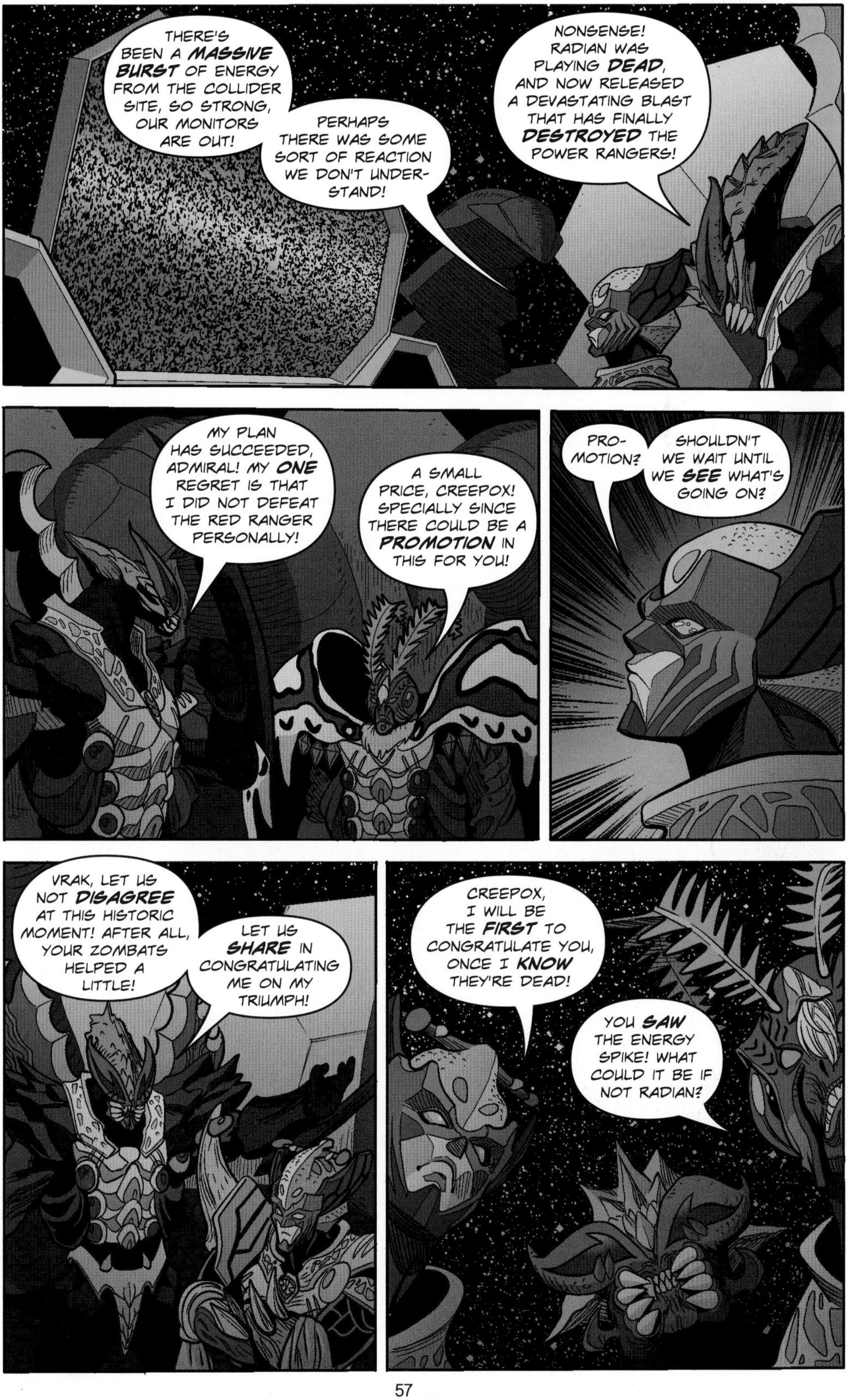
THERE'S BEEN A MASSIVE BURST OF ENERGY FROM THE COLLIDER SITE, SO STRONG, OUR MONITORS ARE OUT!
PERHAPS THERE WAS SOME SORT OF REACTION WE DON'T UNDER-STAND!
NONSENSE! RADIAN WAS PLAYING DEAD, AND NOW RELEASED A DEVASTATING BLAST THAT HAS FINALLY DESTROYED THE POWER RANGERS!
MY PLAN HAS SUCCEEDED, ADMIRAL! MY ONE REGRET IS THAT I DID NOT DEFEAT THE RED RANGER PERSONALLY!
A SMALL PRICE, CREEPOX! SPECIALLY SINCE THERE COULD BE A PROMOTION IN THIS FOR YOU!
PRO-MOTION?
SHOULDN'T WE WAIT UNTIL WE SEE WHAT'S GOING ON?
VRAK, LET US NOT DISAGREE AT THIS HISTORIC MOMENT! AFTER ALL, YOUR ZOMBATS HELPED A LITTLE!
LET US SHARE IN CONGRATULATING ME ON MY TRIUMPH!
CREEPOX, I WILL BE THE FIRST TO CONGRATULATE YOU, ONCE I KNOW THEY'RE DEAD!
YOU SAW THE ENERGY SPIKE! WHAT COULD IT BE IF NOT RADIAN?

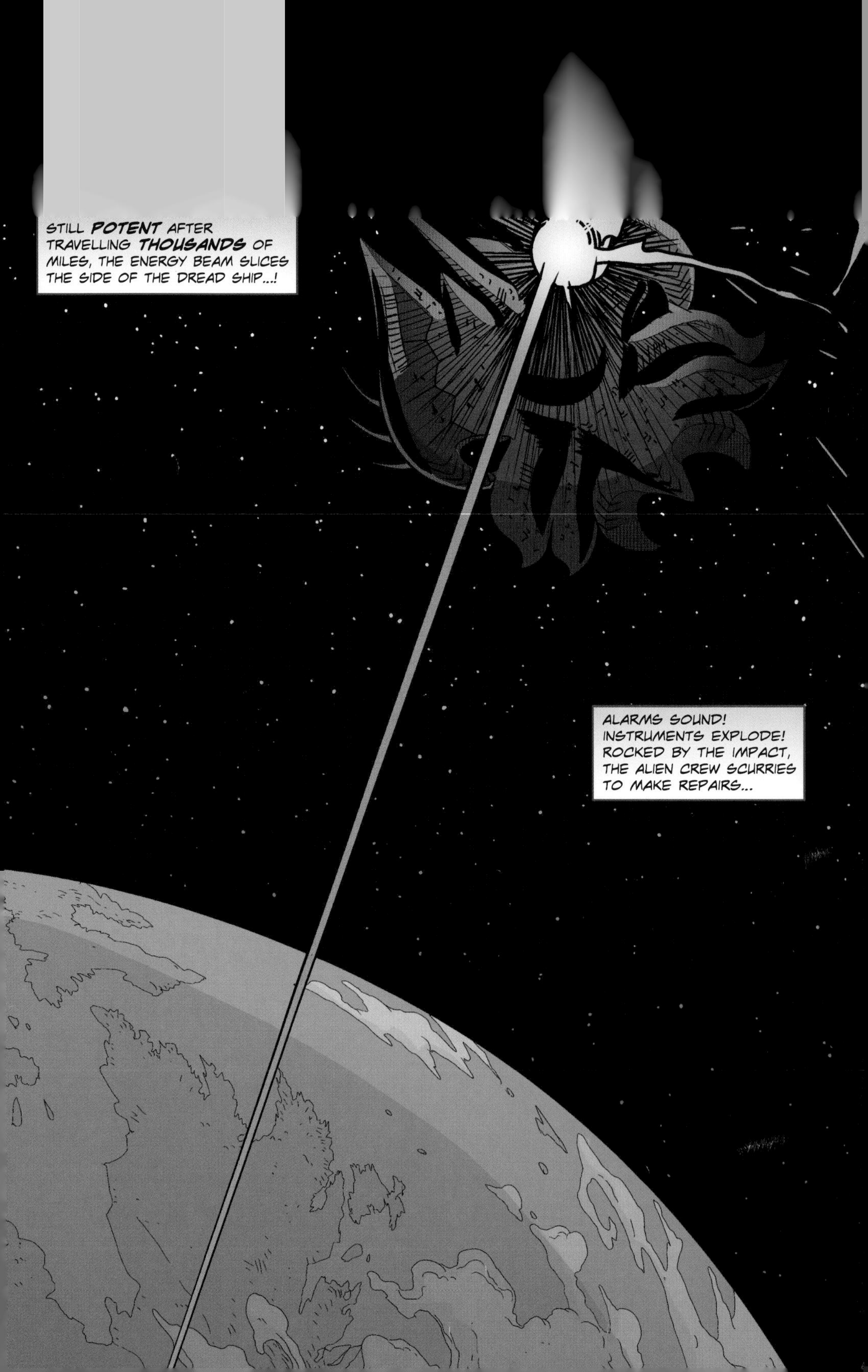
STILL POTENT AFTER TRAVELLING THOUSANDS OF MILES, THE ENERGY BEAM SLICES THE SIDE OF THE DREAD SHIP...!
ALARMS SOUND! INSTRUMENTS EXPLODE! ROCKED BY THE IMPACT, THE ALIEN CREW SCURRIES TO MAKE REPAIRS...

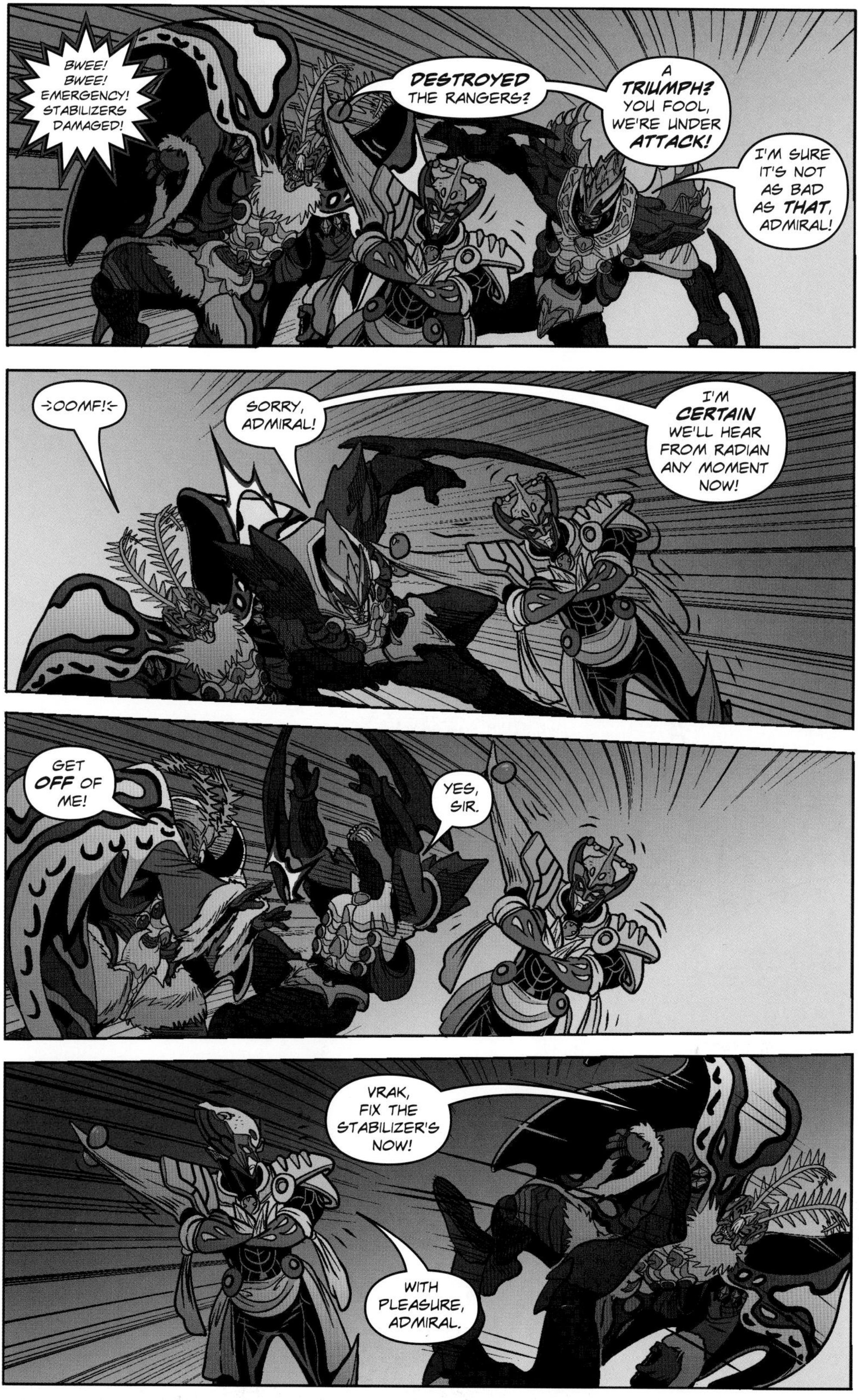
BWEE! BWEE! EMERGENCY! STABILIZERS DAMAGED!
DESTROYED THE RANGERS?
A TRIUMPH? YOU FOOL, WE'RE UNDER ATTACK!
I'M SURE IT'S NOT AS BAD AS THAT, ADMIRAL!
OOMF!
SORRY, ADMIRAL!
I'M CERTAIN WE'LL HEAR FROM RADIAN ANY MOMENT NOW!
GET OFF OF ME!
YES, SIR.
VRAK, FIX THE STABILIZER'S NOW!
WITH PLEASURE, ADMIRAL.

AS THE WARSTAR SHIP STRUGGLES, BACK ON EARTH...

IT'S NOAH!

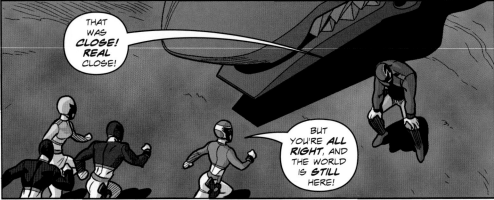

THAT WAS **CLOSE! REAL** CLOSE!

BUT YOU'RE **ALL RIGHT**, AND THE WORLD IS **STILL** HERE!

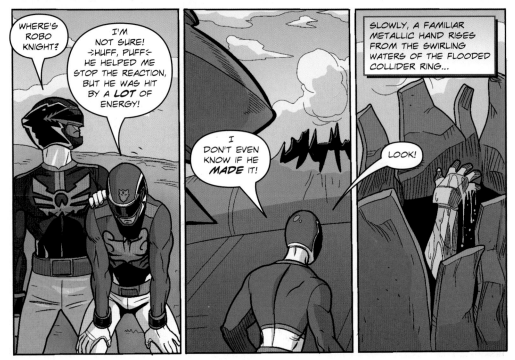

WHERE'S ROBO KNIGHT?

I'M NOT SURE! ⇒HUFF, PUFF⇐ HE HELPED ME STOP THE REACTION, BUT HE WAS HIT BY A **LOT** OF ENERGY!

I DON'T EVEN KNOW IF HE **MADE** IT!

SLOWLY, A FAMILIAR METALLIC HAND RISES FROM THE SWIRLING WATERS OF THE FLOODED COLLIDER RING...

LOOK!

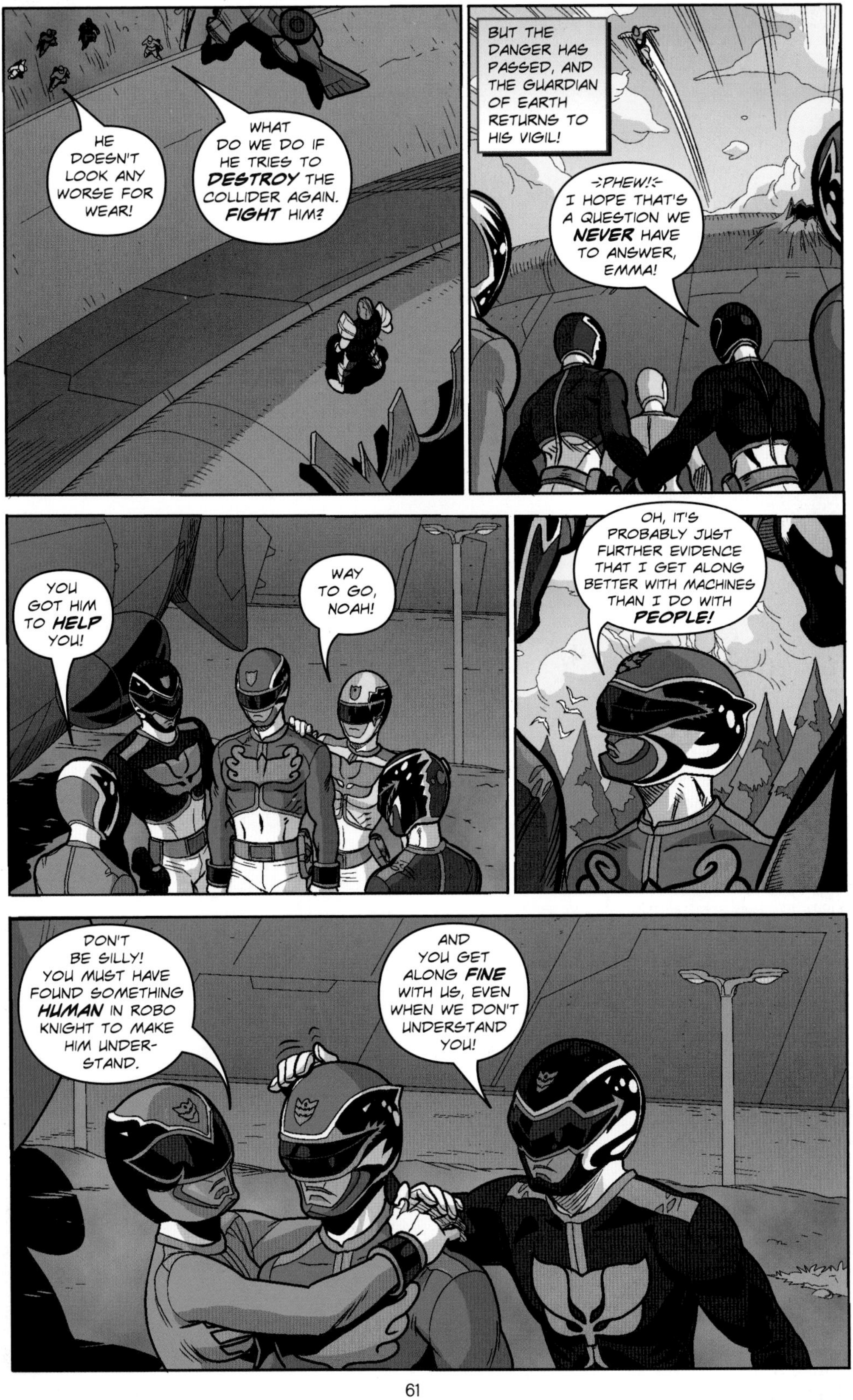
HE DOESN'T LOOK ANY WORSE FOR WEAR!
WHAT DO WE DO IF HE TRIES TO DESTROY THE COLLIDER AGAIN. FIGHT HIM?
BUT THE DANGER HAS PASSED, AND THE GUARDIAN OF EARTH RETURNS TO HIS VIGIL!
PHEW! I HOPE THAT'S A QUESTION WE NEVER HAVE TO ANSWER, EMMA!
YOU GOT HIM TO HELP YOU!
WAY TO GO, NOAH!
OH, IT'S PROBABLY JUST FURTHER EVIDENCE THAT I GET ALONG BETTER WITH MACHINES THAN I DO WITH PEOPLE!
DON'T BE SILLY! YOU MUST HAVE FOUND SOMETHING HUMAN IN ROBO KNIGHT TO MAKE HIM UNDER-STAND.
AND YOU GET ALONG FINE WITH US, EVEN WHEN WE DON'T UNDERSTAND YOU!

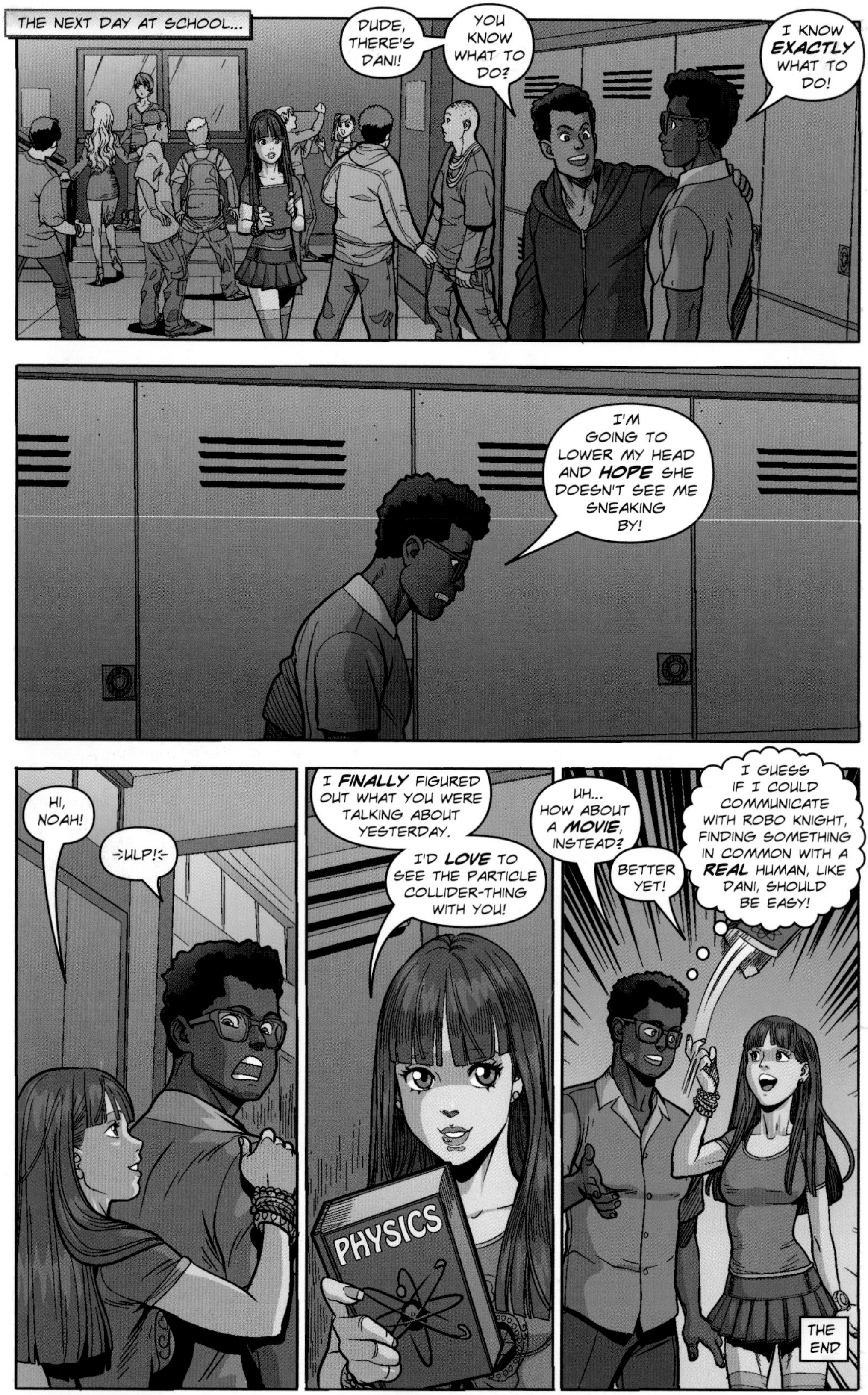
THE NEXT DAY AT SCHOOL...
DUDE, THERE'S DANI!
YOU KNOW WHAT TO DO?
I KNOW EXACTLY WHAT TO DO!
I'M GOING TO LOWER MY HEAD AND HOPE SHE DOESN'T SEE ME SNEAKING BY!
HI, NOAH!
-ULP!-
I FINALLY FIGURED OUT WHAT YOU WERE TALKING ABOUT YESTERDAY.
I'D LOVE TO SEE THE PARTICLE COLLIDER-THING WITH YOU!
PHYSICS
UH... HOW ABOUT A MOVIE, INSTEAD?
BETTER YET!
I GUESS IF I COULD COMMUNICATE WITH ROBO KNIGHT, FINDING SOMETHING IN COMMON WITH A REAL HUMAN, LIKE DANI, SHOULD BE EASY!
THE END

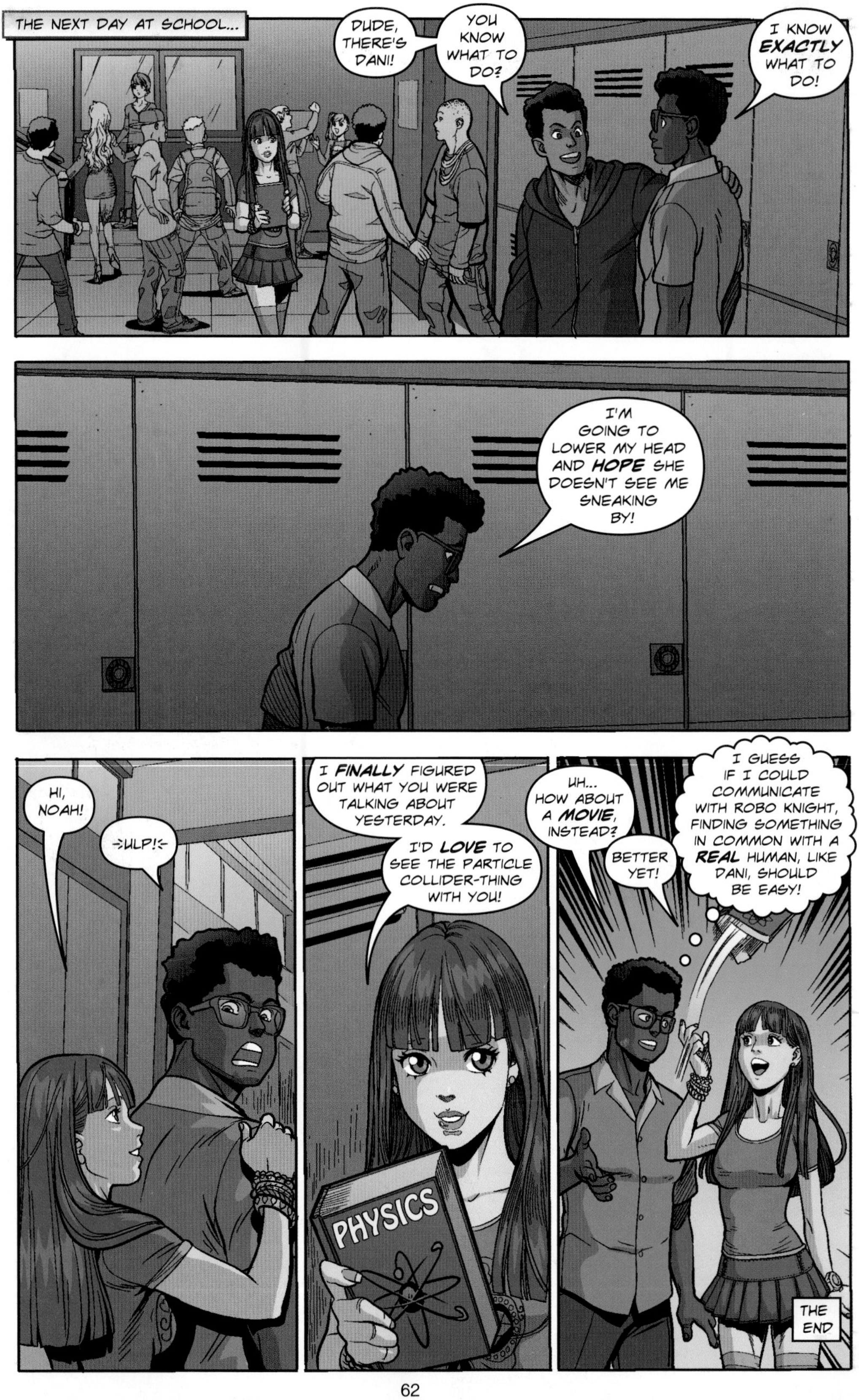
THE NEXT DAY AT SCHOOL...
DUDE, THERE'S DANI!
YOU KNOW WHAT TO DO?
I KNOW EXACTLY WHAT TO DO!
I'M GOING TO LOWER MY HEAD AND HOPE SHE DOESN'T SEE ME SNEAKING BY!
HI, NOAH!
>ULP!<
I FINALLY FIGURED OUT WHAT YOU WERE TALKING ABOUT YESTERDAY.
I'D LOVE TO SEE THE PARTICLE COLLIDER-THING WITH YOU!
PHYSICS
UH... HOW ABOUT A MOVIE, INSTEAD?
BETTER YET!
I GUESS IF I COULD COMMUNICATE WITH ROBO KNIGHT, FINDING SOMETHING IN COMMON WITH A REAL HUMAN, LIKE DANI, SHOULD BE EASY!
THE END

WATCH OUT FOR PAPERCUTZ™

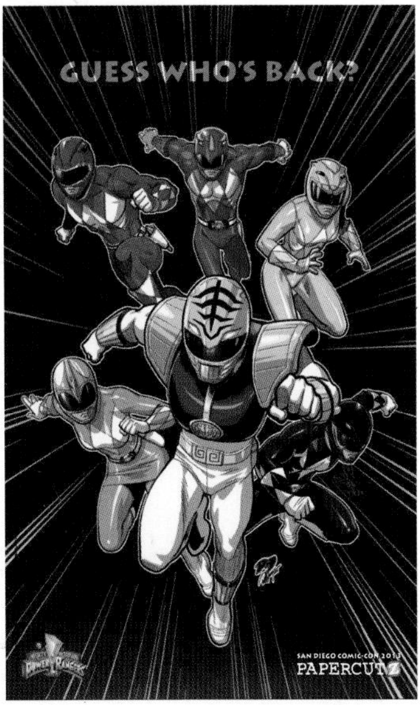
GUESS WHO'S BACK?
SAN DIEGO COMIC-CON 2013
PAPERCUTZ

Welcome to the fantastic, fact-filled fourth SABAN'S POWER RANGERS MEGAFORCE graphic novel from Papercutz. Though technically, this is actually the second MEGAFORCE graphic novel, as the first two POWER RANGERS graphic novels were devoted to the SUPER SAMURAI team. In any case, they were all from Papercutz, the friendly folks dedicated to publishing great graphic novels for all-ages. I'm Jim Salicrup, the positive strangelet who happens to be the Gosei-like Editor-in-Chief of Papercutz, here with a few news items you may enjoy...

As we morphed from a series of POWER RANGERS SUPER SAMURAI graphic novels into a series of POWER RANGERS MEGAFORCE graphic novels, there was also a subtle change amongst our creative crew. Specifically, Paulo Henrique, the artist on the first series, was replaced by someone who draws remarkably like him, named PH Marcondes. Well, the reason for the startling similar art style is that Paulo Henrique and PH Marcondes are actually one and the same! Paulo simply prefers to be known as PH, and we're willing to do almost anything to keep such a super-talented artist as happy as possible (especially when it doesn't cost us anything extra.)!

Now, if you're a POWER RANGERS fan who follows all the POWER RANGERS news and developments online, then you're probably already aware of our next bit of really BIG NEWS. This year, at the COMIC-CON® INTERNATIONAL: SAN DIEGO, we announced that in honor of the 20th Anniversary of the POWER RANGERS we would be bringing back to comics the original MIGHTY MORPHIN POWER RANGERS! That's right, due to popular demand, we'll be presenting an all-new, never before seen tale of THE MIGHTY MORPHIN POWER RANGERS! No sooner did we drop that little bombshell on an unsuspecting public, the Internet was abuzz—spreading the word far and wide that Papercutz was actually listening to the thousands of fans that suggested that we do just that! Hey, we'd be crazy not to! That's why we run that little "Stay In Touch" box on all these "Watch Out for Papercutz" pages—so that we can hear from you! You tell us what you want, and we'll do everything we possibly can to give it to you! Or in this case, Stefan Petrucha, PH (or who knows what his name will be next?) Marcondes, Laurie E. Smith, Bryan Senka, and Michael Petranek—the creative team supreme will do it!

We actually had another major announcement at Comic-Con—that we'll be publishing all-new comics based on the WWE, written by 3-time WWE Champion and New York Times bestselling author Mick Foley—but we're sure you know all about it, if you're keeping your eye on our wacky website!

Whew! That's enough exciting announcements for now. Let's just all agree to pick up this conversation in SABAN'S MIGHTY MORPHIN POWER RANGERS #1, shall we? Until then, don't ever forget those immortal words of many a great hero—"Go, go, Power Rangers!"

Thanks,

Jim

STAY IN TOUCH!

EMAIL:	salicrup@papercutz.com
WEB:	www.papercutz.com
TWITTER:	@papercutzgn
FACEBOOK:	PAPERCUTZGRAPHICNOVELS
SNAIL MAIL:	Papercutz, 160 Broadway, Suite 700, East Wing, New York, NY 10038

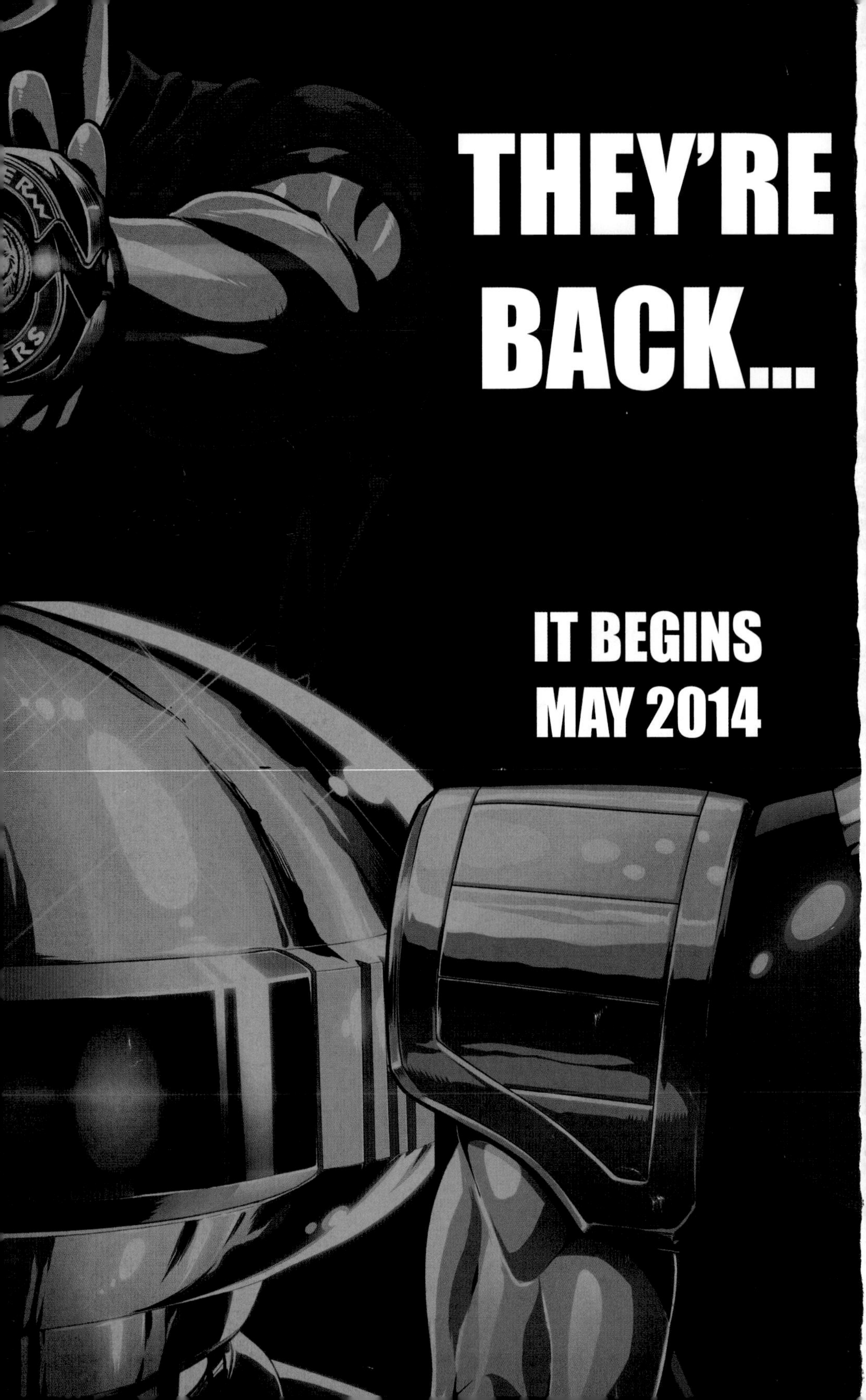
THEY'RE BACK...
IT BEGINS
MAY 2014

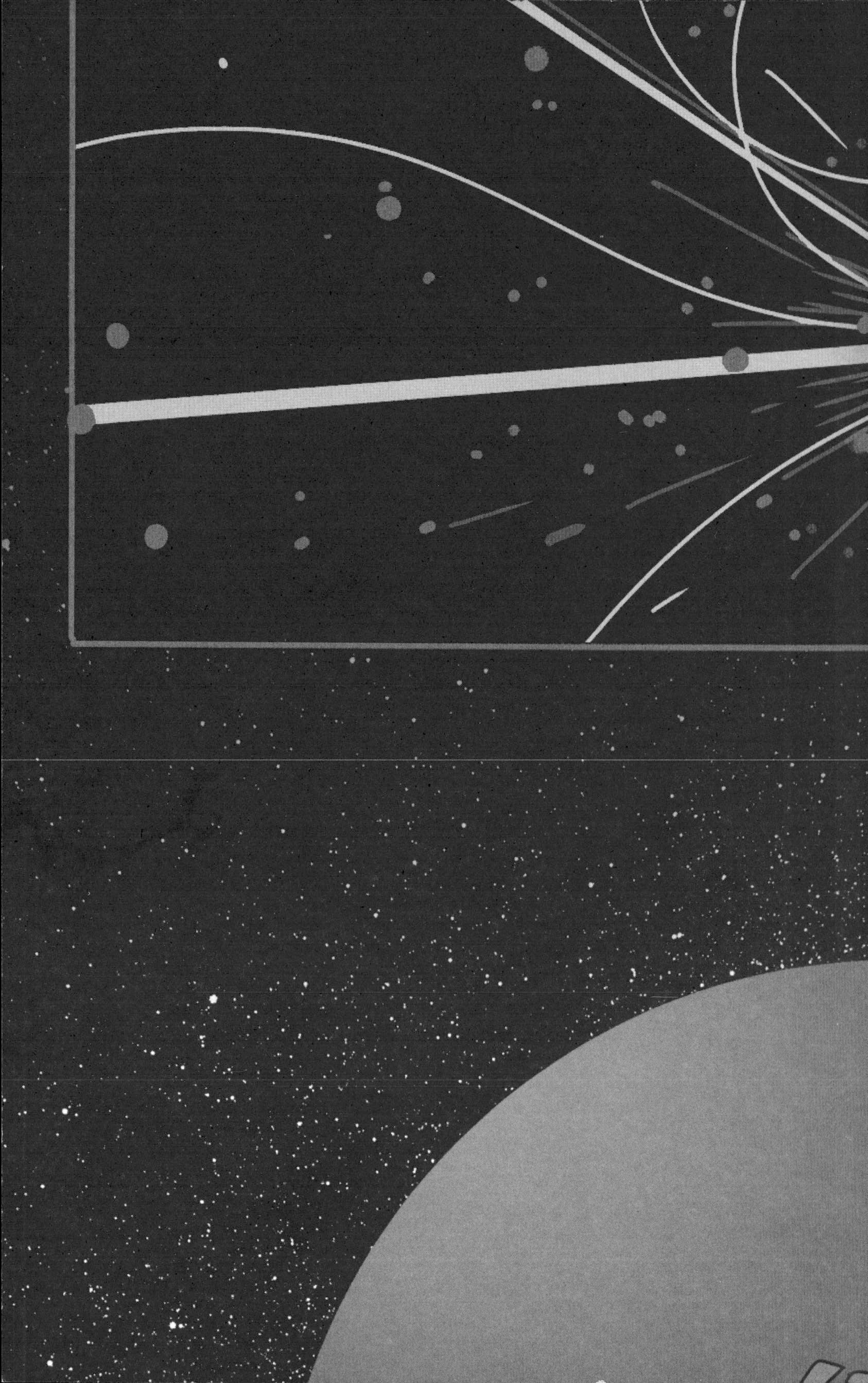